# GIANT'S MOUNTAIN

Jeffrey J. Michaels

# GIANT'S MOUNTAIN

Printed in the United States of America
First Printing – November 2023

Original cover painting by Lane Brown
ISBN #   978-0-9969371-7-7

To all the children
who seek light

To T.,O.,K.,F., and L.

And always, Jill

Table of Contents

# 1

# GIANT'S MOUNTAIN

FOUR CHILDREN WHO HAD NEVER SEEN THE SUN noticed
the peak of Giant's Mountain. Pale light seeped through
thick clouds. Patches of gray snow soaked up what sparse
light fell upon the ground. Today, wind blew, and fog
shifted. The mountain stood revealed. Wind shifted, and
fog drifted, and the mountain once more returned to the
shrouded land of legend. Except...

They had seen it with their own seven eyes.

The world changes in such ways: a puff of air that
smells of land, the glimpse of a far-away sea, the notion of
a place unheard of, yet possible. These children, those four
and one other, decided to change their world that day.
They did not know that. What they really decided was to
find and climb Giant's Mountain. What the boy Micha
desired was to save his dying village.

Until that day, Giant's Mountain had been unseen.
Tales were told, once-upon-a-time tales, and many of those
tales took place because of the Giant King. The lore of the
mountain was a presence in the children's lives, theirs and
their parents and grandparents back into misty memory.

The presence, though, was one of story, an essence, a thing that no longer existed. Except…

It did.

It was not a golden mountain, as the old fables would have it. It did not have a green path winding about from bottom to top like a vine. It did not appear to be what they knew it to be, but it *was* that thing. In their young hearts they were certain. Each one knew it in the moment of first sight. Each felt the truth of the knowledge in their hearts. Only Camber did not know or feel the truth.

Camber went along because he was in trouble. Again.

"You didn't see any Giant's Mountain," Camber said.

"Don't believe? Don't follow." Micha, the oldest of the four, but younger than Camber by a year's turning, did not look back when he spoke. His grey eyes remained fixed on the spot where he saw the mountain. He did not want to lose the vision or the way. They were three days out from their village and already in bigger trouble than Micha expected.

"Better pick sling stones. You'll be hungry if you don't." From behind him Para sent her voice directly to Camber's left ear. Then she shifted to his right. "Better spare your water. River's tomorrow. We started too late today."

Camber looked back in annoyance, left then right. "Who are you to tell me what to do?"

Para slung a stone past Camber's nose. It made a high-pitched hum, then a soft pat. Camber dodged needlessly. "Watch it!" he complained.

Para stepped off the rough path, walking several paces into the wet woods. She bent down. When she stood again, one hand held the squirrel she'd hit with her stone. The other hand held the stone.

"I have dinner," she said. "What do you have?" Hopping back onto the path, Para maneuvered herself to be behind Micha, skipping lightly to catch up. Camber stood still, lips pressed together.

"Don't stop!" Persa pressed past Camber, nearly pushing him off the narrow game path. Tymon followed close behind. Now Camber was last in line, a line that moved away from him at a good pace.

Micha was tall and dressed in deer leather he himself crafted. Para, lean and lithe, wore a similar outfit, crafted the same way, a gift from Micha, no doubt. She barely came to Micha's shoulders, her dark hair in a long braid. They carried packs larger than the two younger children who followed them. Persa looked much like her sister Para, though Persa had not yet taken on the shape of a woman. Tymon, just a bit younger than Persa, was already broader of shoulder than the girl, though shorter by a little.

Persa and Tymon wore the same clothes that all the village children wore. Cloth jerkins and breeches. Camber recalled those jerkins from his own youth. Not much for warmth, but the hike seemed to keep the children warm. They had cloaks wrapped about their shoulders. He noticed their feet were shod in the same style deerskin boots as Micha and Para. Again, no doubt Micha's work. The village sandals would not be of much use in the forest, especially not on such a long trek.

Camber wore his father's hunting boots.

Glancing about, Camber saw two good-sized stones and swept them into his sling pouch. Smooth from an ancient flood, the stones were too big to travel fast, but Camber had the strength to use them well. He set off after the four.

A cloth wrapped about Tymon's head trailed down his neck and back as it unraveled. Camber briefly thought of offering to adjust it for him. Before he could act, Persa slowed a little and brought her hands up to the boy's bandage, tightening and tying, speaking words of empathy and encouragement. Camber hung back and watched, a sullen expression clouding his face.

************

Daylight faded slowly. They had never seen a sunset. The sight of the sun was almost as mythical as Giant's Mountain. Warmth was not something they spoke of except in reference to a hearth fire. They lived in a cold, gray world. It was all they knew except for stories told by others. Camber raised his water skin to his lips, letting a few drops roll onto his tongue. Even their water was cold and gray, he thought, recalling the source of his supply.

Micha led them off the game path and into a sheltered, reasonably dry clearing. Tymon, who had collected twigs and sticks along the way, now gathered larger branches, and built a fire. The others fanned out into the woods, collecting, gathering, returning, dropping their gleanings of fuel near the crackly blaze to dry. Micha sliced wide pine boughs from tall firs, muttering gentle incantations of apology and appreciation to the trees. Camber joined him, and together they built a crude but effective shelter near invisible in the woods.

Para and Persa skinned and gutted three scrawny squirrels and a boney rabbit. Skewering them, they set the meat to cooking above Tymon's fire. The cloth covering his eye once again showed a red stain. A tear of blood slid down his cheek.

Persa sat next to him and pulled the rag from his head. An ugly cut ran from his scalp down across his left eye curving towards his ear. The blood was clotted in many areas, but the cut was deepest across the eye. "You may not see from it again." Persa spoke to Tymon matter of fact. The boy shook his head slightly in acknowledgement.

"I was careless," he said.

"You saved us," Persa replied.

"One bandit will be no more trouble to anyone, thanks to you." Para sidled up to the youngster. "You were quicker than I was, that's for sure. He was too close for me to get a sling bead. I was too slow to pull my knife. But for your quick action, we'd all be dead, and no one would know." She peered at his wound.

Preest told them they were so and so many years old. In the village, Preest counted days and kept track of things like that. Tymon, he said, was nine years old. Micha at fifteen would soon join the men for regular hunting of larger game. Para envied him this, but Preest said tradition would not allow a woman to bring blood to the hunt. At fourteen Para was to be useful to the community within the village walls.

These numbers meant little to them. Each day was the same as the last. Life changed little, and the weather did the same. Until the morning they saw the mountain.

"What happened to you?" Camber made a move to join the three but stayed just a bit separate. He knew they did not like him much. It would be smart to wait for an invitation to join in.

"You care? About someone else?" Para did not look at him. She poured some clean water from her water skin onto the rag and brushed gently at Tymon's wound. Persa chewed some leaves and packed them into a mass which she pressed against his forehead and temple. Tymon winced at the pressure but never cried out, never pulled away.

"We're of a tribe," Camber replied. "We stay together."

"Then why are you out alone? You're in trouble with your da again, right?" Para's tone was derisive, but only slightly so. It didn't do to talk about the elders with disrespect. The village population was small these days and getting smaller. Camber did not reply. He looked away.

Micha came and stood over the younger kids. "Leave him be, Para. He built the shelter for us." Para knew that Camber only helped Micha but chose not to make a point. She was not inclined to disagree with Micha these days, though once upon a time they fought each other like wolf cubs over scrap meat.

Micha knelt and looked Tymon in his good eye. "Hurt?" he asked.

"A little," Tymon replied.

"More than that I wager, but you're being strong. It's good to be strong but tell us what you need. Right?" Tymon nodded agreement to Micha's words. Micha continued, "That was quite a bit of bravery, and you're still being brave. You are one of the battlecrafters now, no denying, and sooner than I. Good deeds, Tymon."

The girls' healing hands and care helped the boy's pain, but those words from Micha set him on the path of recovery. Micha turned to Camber. Both boys stood up. Slightly younger and slightly taller, Micha tipped his head, and the two walked away from the three.

When they were alone, Micha said, "Your father's boots." Camber shivered and looked at his feet. Micha said, "Can you move in them? Silent?"

"They fit fine and are well suited to stalking. I will not give us away."

"There may be more to this conversation between us in the future, but let it be only between us." Micha held out his arm. Camber gripped Micha's wrist as Micha did his. They stood silent a moment, then, "Camber, we need more white bark for Tymon's badge. He'll have some pain this night and that is truth. We're losing light. I know you know the night. If you miss the camp, whistle this way." Micha sounded three notes and then two. "I'll take watch until you return. There is a high patch of ground just that way. There will be a stand of white peelers there. Bring as much as you can carry. We'll save you some meat."

Camber nodded and accepted the task by moving in the direction indicated.

Micha spoke low to the others. With a little movement of his thumb, he pointed towards Camber's retreating sounds. "His sire tried to kill him. He told me when I found him this morning. He got chased from town. His own father banished his own son from his house. When we return, we'll have to deal with that. Until then, Camber is with us." Micha did not ask a question. Para did not nod in agreement but stayed silent. "You haven't looked at him," he said to her. "You haven't seen his bruises."

"I've seen *my* bruises," Para said, looking away. "There is more to his story that he is not telling."

Pressing his lips together as Para turned away, Micha turned back to the wounded boy. "Tymon, when Camber returns, we'll make a brew, and you'll swallow it. We'll make it thick and sticky. It will taste horrible. You'll choke on it. You'll wish you were fighting the bandit again." Micha smiled, and Tymon gave a little grin in return. "But then you'll sleep, and in the day the swelling and pain will be less."

"Tomorrow we reach the river." Para's voice, soft as always, brought the thought they all were thinking into words. "No one crosses the river. The Others live there. What if the mountain…"

Micha made a sharp, cutting motion with his hand. He said, "We talked about this. If you don't want to go, then turn back now. You can live well on your own. You are good in the forest, and you know how to find our tracks to get back home. I'll find you when I come back." Micha spoke directly without emotion, but Para sensed his disappointment at the thought of her leaving. At least she hoped he was disappointed at that thought.

Para replied sharply, "I'm not leaving, only saying. Now we have Camber and a wounded one." She hesitated just a little, then said, "I will keep the wounded one before Camber."

"All or none. That is what we said when we saw the mountain." Micha looked at them all. He sat between them and the fire, his face shadowed. Five bright firelit eyes looked back and there was no fear in any of them.

"Camber didn't see it," Para said. "Only us. I'll do as you say, Micha. You know I will, and Persa and Tymon too. We are one. But now we are one and one other. I will do as you say, but I will be watching your back."

Micha looked her in the eye. She did not flinch, and he did not wish it. "You would do so in all times. It is what I expect. Watch all our backs, Para." He turned away from them and looked into the darkening wood. Camber would be some time. "Eat. Then rest and sleep if you can. Leave some food. I will watch." He looked back at Tymon. "I will wake you when the foul brew is ready. You will hate me for it."

"I will stay watch with you until Camber returns." Tymon's voice was hopeful.

"You will rest." Micha commanded the boy, moving away from the three. Long shadows closed around him.

After a meal of cooked meat and some berries, a few swallows of water gathered from an icy pond three days past, some winter moss packed beneath the bandage against Tymon's wound, the three curled together for warmth in the rough pine-bough shelter.

# 2
# CREATURES IN THE DARK

CAMBER WALKED IN THE NIGHT BRIGHT. He knew that the light came from Moon. Preest told them so, and the children knew of the cycles of Moon even though it remained unseen above the ever-present clouds. Lately the night brightness was more intense. Some months a person could find their way about the rough streets without a torch to light the way. Most did not know this. Most did not venture out at night under any circumstances.

Camber knew. He often found himself safer outside than in. His da would take to the barrel, so Camber would take to the streets. It was not a way for a young man to exist. It was not good for him to be outcast. The elders would listen to none of his grievances. His father was a long-time leader of the hunters. The village needed hunters more than ever.

Camber's mother was not a person he carried in clear memory. He did recall the final time he saw her. The recollections arrived mostly in frightening dreams. He shook his head, clearing away useless thoughts. Focus on the task at hand, he said to himself.

The white peelers stood out in the copse at the top of a rise. Moon glow brightened the ever-present clouds, and the trees reflected this pale light. From the rise, he had a good view of the surrounding area. Despite it being night, the shapes and depth of shadows could convey much information.

Off to the right, a silver strand of light indicated the river. If they walked south a bit, they could arrive early in the morning. Camber would mention this but knew Micha would choose to continue the northeast course. They would meet the river late in the day, perhaps even the next morning, and for the four it would be enough. Camber's water skin was nearly empty. Mouthfuls of grimy snow kept him going, but he thirsted for clean water.

Somehow, Micha and the others convinced themselves they knew where Giant's Mountain was located. It was a dangerous delusion and surprised Camber. Micha and Para were too practical, too level-headed to get involved in this kind of fool's journey. Camber wanted to doubt, but they seemed so certain of their vision. Long had Micha spoken of how the village was failing and what they might do to save it from ruin. Camber never found the time to join in with their idealistic dreaming. Were they so desperate they now pursued myth and fable in the hopes of a miracle? But what did he have to lose by accompanying them? Micha was the closest thing to a friend Camber had. Even then, he knew Micha would side with Para against him if he stepped out of line.

Camber pulled long swaths of bark from the trees while he pondered the geography and his situation. He could not return to the village. Even when they did, he could not accompany them. There was a fact he had left out of the story he'd told Micha.

Camber muttered similar incantations to the trees as Micha had when cutting the pine boughs. He asked for their favor and strength to heal another being. He reminded the trees that part of their purpose was to supply to the animals of the forest. He offered to give some of his blood if they so desired. No thorns caught his flesh. No sharp twigs pricked his skin. The trees were pleased that they would be put to good use.

Something caught his eye as he was about to leave. There, on the far side of the river, not far from the edge, a brief flash of firelight glowed in the mist. In the heavy night air, he strained his ears for a glimpse of sound. Wind rose up, and a patch of rain sped in sharp angles through the forest around him. The night grew darker. Light vanished from the clouds.

He would mention this also. Micha may not be aware that the Others are so close. None of the children ever ventured this far from their home, not even in hunting parties. None would willingly travel to the Others' territory. This added to the puzzle of Micha and the odd quest.

The sky looked lighter back towards the direction of the camp. Camber stood in the shelter of a tall tree and chose to wait until the rain passed. It did not last long. As he gathered his harvest, he looked northeast. There, a great bulk of shadow stood, high and wide and taller than any other mountain Camber had seen. At the very top, a slight, golden light glowed. He watched for more than a few moments before the shadowy form faded into darkness. The light also vanished. The dark that followed was suddenly frightening and almost unbearable.

He had seen the mountain! All their lives and the life of the village, legends about a time when the world was ruled by the Giant King were spoken, argued, believed, and doubted. Some villagers said the tales were all true, but Camber felt the stories were too fabulous to be so. Some said they were all false, but the artifacts Preest kept clearly spoke of a very different time and culture. One with giants? Perhaps.

Camber traveled quickly through the dark wood. He caused slight noises, but only those that could be mistaken for wind through leaves. He whistled his approach, three notes, then two. Micha echoed the final two. They met again in the darkness.

"I believe you," Camber said. "I believe you have seen the mountain." Micha said nothing as he led the way to camp. Wood smoke scented the area. Embers dimly lit the way to the remnants of the meat. Camber pulled a piece to his lips. "I've seen the river too. It is close, but the fires of the Others are near to the shore." He thought a moment, then said, "I could take some of the skins and fill them. I could catch up to you. You'll move slower with Tymon today."

Micha took the bark and began grinding it in a small wooden bowl. He poured a few drops from his own water skin into the mash, mixing some mossy growth and a pinch of dried leaves from his medicine pouch. "Better if he rested the day. This is a good place. Can you find the river in the dark?"

"Slow going for silence, but yes."

Micha brought the thick mix over to the sleeping Tymon. Para and Persa woke at his approach. They'd rested protectively on either side of the wounded boy. Now they cradled and supported him between them.

"Tymon, don't wake up too much. Just open your mouth and let the mix slip down your throat. If it touches your tongue, you'll hate me for certain."

"I can't hate you, Micha," Tymon spoke sleepily. He opened his mouth without opening his eye. The bowl pressed against his lower lip, and he tilted his head to receive the sticky mash. When it dropped into his mouth he gagged and choked. Para clamped her hand against his jaw and forced his mouth closed. He had no choice but to swallow. Tymon struggled against her, but all joined in to hold him still. All but Camber.

"Easy, hero. Just relax and let it slide down the throat." Micha spoke soft and low, adding a little incantation. Tymon stopped fighting but still coughed and choked against Para's hand. She released her grip slowly and stroked the boy's cheek. Tymon made retching noises but kept the mix down. "For your own good, Tymon," Micha said.

"I'll do you the same good one day, Micha." Tymon's voice was bitter but not rude.

Camber came forward. "Here Tymon, drink." There was not much water left in his skin, and he freely allowed Tymon to swallow the lot. Para watched. Camber turned to Micha. "I'll take mine and Tymon's. You keep the other three skins in case I don't get back."

Micha nodded. "You'll get back. You're good at being unseen. Take mine too." He unslung the flaccid skin and tilted it against Tymon's lips. The boy was nearly asleep again but drank the remaining swallow readily.

Handing the empty skin to Camber, Micha said, "You come back here, and we'll all rest." Micha sighed, looking upwards in the direction they traveled. "You saw it? You really did?"

"Just the shadow, but there was a light at the top. They vanished together. I saw it Micha, no lie. The light, it was golden, but not like they say in the stories, not bright and shining. And not the whole mountain, only the top. Pale, like an ember, but golden. Not yellow. Not orange." Camber looked at Micha in the deep shadows of the camp.

Sniffing as Camber spoke, Para tended to Tymon. Persa helped the boy lie back on the bed of pine needles. Para pulled her water skin closer to her and lay down with Tymon. Persa followed, and they pulled their cloaks together over each other.

Camber stood and gathered Tymon and Micha's water skins. "Back just after dawn, Micha. Promise."

"Don't take chances, Camber. Stay away from the Others. We'll go thirsty if we need to, but come back safe and quiet, right?"

"I'll be back. With full skins." And with that he faded into the dark wood.

*************

Night closed about him. He crept through shadows by instinct. Camber was good with shadows. It worried him. Preest told of shadow creatures, men like beasts who turned and killed for no good reason. Preest said they weren't born as such but became the beast when they left childhood. Camber did not always believe old Preest, but in this he did. His own father was one of them, a beast man. Or so Camber believed. The village elders would hear none of it. Soon, by the counting of Preest, Camber would be leaving childhood.

Time was kept somewhere inside him. He knew he was close to the river by the time spent travelling. Land sloped down, and trees thinned. Rocks, exposed by old floods, began to appear about the land. He slowed. Slipping on mossy stone would twist an ankle or knee.

Camber slid forward slower and slower. Always a tree trunk between him and the river. Always a listening ear before a step. The water flowed quickly here and spoke a lively tale. He slid his eye around a tilting oak.

Moon above clouds must be circling away now. Preest said it moved around the sky. Camber neither believed nor disbelieved this. First, he would have to see Moon to believe.

Dark filled the curved river valley. In deeper shadows the water flowed, and Camber crouched to approach. No light, no fire, no torch, no scent from the Others. No sound, no speech, no ancient language could be detected. Only the river and its song.

Camber found a flat shelf of rock where the river passed close. He lay flat on his belly. Each water skin was submerged in turn, filling and swelling with icy, winter water. Except it should not be winter. Preest said it is summer, but with no sun to touch Gaia, warmth never arrives. Snows were scarce now at the lower slopes and valleys, but mountains held bright white peaks. Except for Giant's Mountain. Camber had seen no snow there. Only the golden light.

Preest told of the time when the village was visited by the Giant King and his companions. They brought blessings and asked for little in return. Build a road here, a bridge there, dig a channel, dig a well, and always the humans were happy to do just so, for the giants then sent fresh water their way or brought visitors and trade into their town square. The giants taught them the secrets of building and the art of metal crafting and forge fires. Preest spoke as if he had been there. He was old, but no one knew his years.

There was magic in what Preest said. At least the village felt it to be magic. They lost the knowledge the giants gave them. Only Preest tried to keep the words. He told the villagers, but they had little time for learning these days. Life was cruel for many. Winter had lasted for many years.

Lost in thought, Camber rested his head against cold, moist stone, his eyes gazing unfocused across the swift stream to shadowed banks, dark under the moon-bright clouds.

Shadows moved. He froze.

Hulking along in a line, four figures moved downstream. In shadow, detail was impossible. Camber allowed his eyes to accept things he could not consciously see. Too-long arms became heavy clubs; shaggy coats became large, antlered heads; broad, hunched backs became deer carcasses. His ears and nostrils joined the sensory search. Whispered voices became the noise of shuffling feet. The smell of blood was present.

They were shorter than he expected. Not as tall as he or Micha. Tymon's height, perhaps. And then they were gone, lost to his sight around the curving river valley. Camber pulled his freezing arm from the water. All feeling was gone from his fingers. Around his wrist was the strap for Tymon's water skin. It was the only reason he still possessed the skin. The boy rolled on his back and tucked his icy hand beneath his rough, furred cloak.

He looked upwards. Clouds parted slightly, and one tiny bright light floated above him. Camber gasped. Moon? No, too small from Preest's stories. What then? Camber searched his memory. Small lights in the night sky…stars? That was right! A star! Clouds filled the gap, and light vanished again. He had seen a star! His heart beat fast. Excitement grew. Caution ebbed. Camber knelt and drank his fill directly from the swift stream. Gathering the three full skins he scrambled back up the slope.

Dull, yellowed eyes peered unblinking from mudbanks downstream.

************

Waning night gave way to grayish dawn. Camber came close to the area of the camp. The wood was not silent.

Birds woke and called their song. Wind picked at branches and dry leaves. Tree boughs sighed and shifted. Moving slow in his approach, Camber was about to whistle, three times then two. He felt Para's blade against his throat. It had been there before. Was she at last going to kill him?

Her voice was a breath of wind, soft against his right ear. "Down. Slow." And they knelt together. She pulled her knife from his throat as they sank to the ground.

"Hiding," Para said, slipping to his left. With a slight movement of her hand, she indicated a direction for Camber to look.

Bushes and branches were thick but winter-dry. Many leaves had fallen away. Despite being summer they had yet to be replenished. Camber gazed past the low foliage in front of them. Subtle movement, large object, human-sized, short, and oddly shaped.

He let his ears open by not listening to the birds and breeze. A frozen crunch, a heavy breath, a muttered word, an answering mutter. Camber released the water skins carefully, letting them slip to the ground. Too close for slings, he drew his knife. Para placed a hand on his arm. "Micha said no," she sighed with the wind. With her hand she held up three fingers. There were three beings. Camber saw they matched his impressions of the Others from earlier in the night.

They were stealthier than he expected. Quiet and swift, they moved through the area, searching and seeking…what? Him? Had he brought them back here? Had they followed? No. They could not have crossed the swift stream in such short time. They were already at the camp when he arrived. Para saved him from walking into them. Camber glanced at the girl. Her lips were pressed tight, eyes bright. She held her blade in readiness. Her body was taut, ready to spring, but she remained still. Still, because Micha told her.

Camber now reached his senses farther outwards. Where was Micha? And Persa? And wounded Tymon? Camber adjusted his body to match Para's readied state. A noise, a scuffle, and some fierce yips drew their attention. It was all so brief and ending fast. Camber looked to Para for direction. She looked back. Camber could see the girl was forcing herself to remain still. She wanted to move, wanted to see the what and where of her friends and family. Micha had told her no, stay still.

Then the Others were gone. They left the area. Camber thought he heard them down the slope but was unsure of direction. A whistle soft and low, two notes then three. Para answered three. She sprang from their hiding place, racing to the camp, Camber following close.

Micha stood, a shadow in the wood. Their small fire was now extinguished and sodden, little puddles amongst the dead coals.

Para ran to him. "Micha are you…"

He caught her in one lean arm and pulled her close. The two held each other a moment, then Micha looked at Camber and said, "They took Tymon. Persa tried to stop them. I told her, 'Stay still.' They took her too." He grabbed Para by her long braid and yanked her head around. "I told you to stay still!"

"OWWW! Stop it!" Para squealed her outrage and twisted away from Micha. "I saw Camber! I saw a way to stop him from getting caught! Did you mean to say, 'Thank you, Para, for not getting caught and for saving Camber?' Is that what you meant to say?" The two leaned toward each other, Para glaring fiercely. Camber thought Para might strike Micha.

"Thank you, Para." Camber spoke low, but firmly. "You may have saved my life."

She turned her ire to him. "I didn't do it for you! I did it so they wouldn't think we were still here. We were hiding, and you came lumbering back up the hill. They would have known we were here if they saw you with three full skins."

Camber's face flushed. "I'm sorry. I wasn't thinking. I saw some of them down by the river last night. I didn't think they would be up here too."

Micha sighed. "You did good, Para. Camber…" Micha frowned. "It's alright. You did not know. How could you? Did you get water? We're going to need it."

"Yes, Micha. Three full skins. What are we going to do?"

"Get Persa and Tymon away from the trolls."

"Trolls!" Para put her hand to her face. Camber shivered. Preest had told them about trolls, had warned them all as children. Stay in town or the trolls will get you. Stay in town and never leave. Behave and obey or the trolls will get you. They will eat you. As children, they believed and feared and obeyed.

Now Camber was older. Micha too. They went on short hunts with the elder men. They heard the elders talk. They heard them laugh about the trolls. No such thing really, they said when the wine skins were empty. The Others, though, they were real. Stay away from their territory.

"Trolls!" Para said again. "They were trolls? Micha, no lying! No scaring, Micha.

"They looked just like Preest described. Short, hairy, wearing skins, and ugly. They grunted and pushed each other about, just like the old stories. Strong too. Big arms and thick short legs. I was scared when I saw them. Is that what you saw, Camber? By the river?"

"Like that, but it was dark and not clear. Are the trolls the Others? Will they…" Camber stopped his words.

"What, Camber? Say it!" Para glared at him. "Will they eat them? My little sister and Tymon, will they be eaten by the trolls?"

Camber felt bad for saying anything. He kept quiet.

"No." Micha spoke firm. "We will get them back, Para. You and me."

"Me too, Micha." Camber's voice was low. "If you'll have me along. I can help. I can."

"This will be hard, Camber. You will be welcome if you wish to help, but I will not ask this of you."

Camber stayed quiet, nodding yes.

"Good then. Grab our water skins. Para, grab Persa's roll. The trolls took her water skin. I'll get Tymon's gear. You both have stones for slings?" They nodded. "Good. Silence is best. I'll lead. Para, follow me at hunter's distance. Camber, you stay a distance from us and keep our backs safe. I've seen you follow on the hunt. You are good at it." Without another word, Micha took to the trolls' trail.

Yellow eyes watched the three youths depart, following their captive friends and captors.

# 3

# TRACKING TROLLS

PERSA SQUIRMED AGAINST LEATHER THONGS. She twisted her face, trying to escape the rank skin strapped across her mouth. It was soft enough but reeked. She was angry. Angry at the trolls for certain, but angry at herself mostly.

Micha told her. Stay still, he said, and she should have listened to Micha. But Para moved, and *she* was alright. She went and saved Camber. That part surprised Persa. Para made no deception about her feelings against Camber.

Micha was smart. He must have sensed the trolls approaching. Micha pulled the sisters back past the border of the camp. He left Tymon in the shadows on the far side, sleeping off the white bark draught. With Para a stone's throw to his left, Micha put Persa closer on his right, and the last thing he said was, "Stay still."

Tymon was well hidden. Micha's woodcraft made their shelter blend in and look natural. But then, Tymon moaned, and the trolls found him. Three trolls grunted to each other. One, then another, looked around trying to find others travelling with the wounded boy. Persa saw them scoop up Tymon, wrapping him tight in his bed roll.

One cradled him like a child. He looked small in the troll's arms.

Persa waited for Micha to attack. The trolls walking away with Tymon was all too much for her. They walked right past her, and she leapt out on the one carrying Tymon. He barely slowed down. The one behind plucked her off his companion's shoulder and bound her while they walked away from the camp. Persa did not make it easy. The troll finally held her by the scruff of her robe and shook her until her head spun. Now, bound and gagged, slung over a troll's shoulder, she looked back down the trail and saw four more trolls joining them.

No Micha. No Para. No Camber. They remained free. She was caught. She should have stayed still. In the future she would always listen to Micha. If there was a future. The anger shared a place in her chest with fear. Persa still attended Preest, who still told tales of the trolls. She believed Preest mostly, but she also believed Para when she said Micha told her there were no trolls. Well, Micha was wrong about this one thing. It made her mad again. She squirmed more.

A large hairy hand grasped her jerkin, lifting her off the troll's shoulder. She hung limp as he held her in front of his scary, hairy face. He moved his mouth about and licked his lips. Persa almost fainted with fear. He shook her a bit, and that made her mad again.

Her legs were bound together at the ankles, but Persa still could swing them, and she did, straight up, her leather-clad heels catching his chin deep under his long beard. The jolt hurt her feet a lot. She watched the troll's face and saw his eyes roll around. He stopped walking and stumbled backwards. The troll following ran into them, and they all tumbled to the ground.

Persa, still bound hand and foot, was now entangled with two very heavy trolls. The leather gag was loose, however, and she let go a high-pitched scream. Birds flew away. Branches shuddered. Ice cracked. The trolls covered their ears, grunting in complaint. Persa was good at screaming. She was a little sister after all. The scream went on for a long time.

Finally, the troll carrying Tymon stomped back towards Persa. He glared at her. He cradled sleeping Tymon and held one large hand over Tymon's right ear, gently pressing the wounded boy's head against his broad chest. "No wake," he said. Persa let the scream expire.

Two other trolls helped the fallen trio to their feet. A new troll grasped Persa by the back of her jerkin and hoisted her up to the level of his face. Not so far from the ground, really, thought Persa. "No screamin'," he said in guttural tones, tossing her across his broad shoulder. The gag was still hanging about her neck, but no one tightened it again.

************

The day passed. For Micha and Para, it was easy to track the trolls. After Persa's scream, they were able to get close and stay close. The trio kept focused on their quarry, catching glimpses of them as the day wore on. Despite being bound and gagged, or, in the case of Tymon, unconscious, the captive children seemed to be alright.

Micha called a halt near dark. A natural hollow against some rocks with a nice overhang made a reasonably comfortable camp. He slipped forward to spy on the trolls, returning to Para and Camber to report.

"There are only seven. They have a fire and are cooking. I can see Persa. She's tied but not gagged. She is next to Tymon. He is awake. The trolls are feeding them."

"But not eating them?" Para asked. She pondered why Micha thought that the number seven was worth an "only" when there were only three of them.

"I saw four of them carrying deer carcasses last night," Camber said. "They are probably eating venison for now. Can we sneak into their camp and get Tymon and Persa back?"

"No and no. They are not eating them, and we can't get into their camp. Too well guarded just now. Anyway, they are not in any danger at the moment."

"Not in danger! They are captured by trolls!" Para leaned close to Micha's face. He put his hand against her cheek. She flinched at first, but relaxed when he touched her gently.

"I know. It won't do us or them any good if we get caught too. I don't know what to do yet, but I will think of something, Para. You know I will." Para calmed down, leaning into Micha's comforting hand.

"I know. You always take care of us, Micha." He slid his arm around her, and she hugged him back.

Embarrassed, Camber shuffled a bit, then said, "Maybe I could get close to their camp and keep a watch, Micha. I can stay up all night and watch for a chance to sneak them out." He paused, then added, "If you think that is a good idea, Micha."

Para leaned back but stayed in Micha's arms. "That is a good idea, Micha! Camber could do that! You say he's good at sneaking about at night. He could do that and not get caught."

Micha looked at Para, then Camber. "There is a lot I do not like about this, but that *is* a good idea, Camber. I don't want you to take any risk of being seen. Stay away from the trolls. If you can get both Persa and Tymon out silently, then good, but only if you get both. Otherwise just keep a watch." He paused, then said, "Maybe that is better. Just keep watch. We'll get some rest here and join you before light. Are you sure you can do this?"

"You know I can, Micha. I'll be careful. I promise."

\*\*\*\*\*\*\*\*\*\*\*\*

Tymon remembered little of how he got here. The horrible paste that Micha and the others forced down his throat did its work well. He slept without pain for a long time. He felt groggy now and wasn't quite sure that he was awake. Tymon slipped in and out of twilight. Persa held his hand. In that state he spoke. His voice remained soft and low. Persa recognized the tale.

"A vine of green rose up to the castle of gold. The giant's mount floats in the clouds. He sees us all and tells us how. We do, and he brings. Once we were few, dying animals and barely human. The giant brought us light, the giant and the dragon. We do not die. The giant asks little."

All around Tymon, squat hairy men wandered to and fro, grunting and cooking and eating and drinking. Micha was not there, or Para, but Persa was sitting right next to him. It looked like she had a beard. He laughed.

Persa turned to look at him, fear further widening her already wide eyes. Tymon's one good eye was half shut, but he saw her look all about before she whispered, "Tymon, it's alright. Stay quiet for now. I am here to help you."

She moved her hands together and Tymon saw the leather straps that bound her wrists. "Persa, how are you going to help me if you are tied up?" The boy shifted and tested his own hands. They were loose and so were his legs. "Maybe I am here to help you." He laughed again, though soft and low.

"Tymon!" Persa whispered fiercely. "Stay quiet! We are captured by trolls!" Tymon's eye snapped open, and he looked all around. Yes, there were hairy trolls all about, and he and Persa were right in the midst of them. He whimpered.

"They didn't get Micha or Para." Persa told what she knew. "Or Camber. Para saved Camber!" Tymon's eye widened in disbelief. Persa had a way of bending the truth, but Para saving Camber? Persa continued. "It is truth. She knocked him down and held his mouth shut so he didn't alert the trolls. But then you moaned in your sleep. They found you. I tried to save you. I got three of them, but there were a dozen others at least. That is how they got me too."

In the back of his mind, Tymon felt there were some gaps in the logic of the tale, but there was a visible truth he could see. Trolls! He hated Preest's stories about trolls. He often lay awake at night listening for the tell-tale sounds of them outside his bedroom wall. Shuffling and snuffling, Preest said, and huffing and puffing. They looked for children, disobedient children mostly, but any would do if they were caught outside at night without their parents. When the children first started sneaking out on the bright nights, Tymon told them, he told them all. Tymon always knew they would get caught by trolls!

Micha tried to set everyone at ease back then. "There are no trolls," he said. "That is only something the elders say to keep us indoors and safe. Anyway, there are other things to be afraid of, if you want to be afraid."

Tymon, the youngest, remembered everything Micha had listed that he could be afraid of. Wolves and bears, night cats and snakes, large owls, because Tymon was still small, and they might just think he was a big mouse. Everybody laughed at that, but Tymon did not. He wanted them to like him. He did not want them to think he was afraid just because he was small. He did not want to be afraid.

Micha talked to him one night. "You can decide to be afraid, or you can decide to be brave. Either way, you have to think clear about things." Micha told him about the hunt, about the charging boar or bear. He said that all men were afraid in those moments, but they thought clear about those things. They thought about those moments when they weren't happening, which was most of the time. They thought about what to do in case of something scary. Tymon loved Micha for those words. He loved Micha for a lot of reasons. No one picked on Tymon because of Micha, and the men let Tymon go along on fishing tramps because of Micha.

Even then, Micha did not want Tymon out with them on Bright Night. Tymon got to come along because of Persa, and Persa got to come along because of Para. Camber, well, he was outside at night a lot. He wasn't really out *with* them, only sometimes he was out when they were.

So Tymon was not afraid of being afraid, and he thought about hunting and swimming and climbing, and he got pretty good at most of it because he was small and light and quiet. Up to now, Tymon trusted Micha. Now there were trolls. Now would be a good time to be afraid, Tymon thought, but think clear.

Tymon loved Persa too, but if they were going to get away they would need more than Persa's imagination. They could not fight the trolls. Tymon still felt weak from the painkilling paste. He felt thirsty too. His wound did not hurt at all, so maybe the vile paste had been worthwhile. He felt his belt, and there was his bone knife, still in the sheath. He kept it sharp, like Micha said. It would cut Persa's bonds easily. Part of thinking clear was keeping your knife sharp.

A shuffling noise made the boy and girl look up. One of the trolls was walking over to them. He held two steaming bowls. Kneeling down, he handed one to Tymon. The scent of the stew suddenly made the boy realize how ravenously hungry he was. He took the stew, and using the little wooden spoon in the bowl, he shoveled the food into his mouth. It was hot and delicious.

The troll set the other bowl down and loosened the leather straps around Persa's wrists. He leaned back on his haunches and pointed to the bowl. Persa was wary. Could this be poisoned stew? Well, it didn't seem to be affecting Tymon poorly. Her friend almost finished his share. She picked up the bowl and ate, tentatively at first, but soon with a gusto that matched Tymon's. When they were finished, the troll handed her a water skin. With a shock, she saw that it was her own.

When she last saw it, it was nearly depleted. She had dripped the remnants of fluid into sleeping Tymon's mouth all through the night as they waited for Camber to return. She and Para had gone without fresh water, sucking on patches of old ice and snow for their share. She was thirsty now and wanted to drink a big swig but knew Tymon must be in worse shape than she. Persa handed the skin first to him.

The troll cocked his head and watched them for a moment. Tymon drank readily but stopped before he drained the skin. "Here, Persa. I'm sorry if I took too much."

"Do you need more? I can be good without water for a while, but you need to build up your strength."

"Thank you, but I'm alright for now." The troll stood up and strolled away, taking their empty food bowls. "He didn't tie you up again," Tymon observed. "Can you undo your legs without anyone seeing?"

"I think so." Persa squirmed her legs underneath her so the binding straps would be hidden while she loosened them. The troll returned bearing two more bowls of food. With the edge off their hunger the two captives had a moment to think about things. Tymon decided to confront the troll.

"Why are you feeding us? Are you fattening us up, so you can eat us later?"

The troll made a confused sound. "Eat," he said, handing them the bowls. "Drink," he said, handing them two full skins.

After they ate and drank, the troll took the bowls and stacked them on the ground. A second member of the troll band approached carrying a staff. Looking down at the two children, he made a whistling noise. The troll that brought the food reached out for Persa's legs. He was fast and pulled the girl's feet until she was lying flat on the ground. Persa yelped. Tymon flew towards the troll, brandishing his knife in the hairy man's face.

In a flash, the troll snatched the knife from Tymon and sliced Persa's bonds. He then handed the knife back, bone handle first. Tymon and Persa looked at each other in confusion.

The troll with the staff dragged it in the dirt, drawing a circle around them. At irregular intervals he put smooth colored stones along the little ditch. "Stay," he said, tapping the staff inside the rough circle. "Sleep." And they left the children alone.

************

Camber was not happy, but he felt good. For the first time in his life, he was being accepted for his abilities. Life in the village faded away for the moment as he crept through the woods towards the troll camp. He felt a little bad at feeling good. Tymon and Persa in the hands of the trolls was not a good thing. But he could help, he knew he could.

And maybe, if he did rescue them, he could be redeemed from…

A shuffling noise came from his left. Camber heard a troll grumbling incoherently. From Camber's right came a cough, then a sneeze, wet and noisy. Camber lay flat, imagining he was a fallen branch. The two trolls walked past him carrying firewood. Without noticing the boy, they walked straight into camp.

Camber lay still for a moment more, then wriggled closer to the perimeter. When he could see clearly into the circle of the troll camp, he paused, making himself more comfortable, pulling old leaves around him for camouflage.

The camp was against a steep and rocky mountain wall. Three small fires, each tended by a troll, flickered in the early night. A fourth troll was cooking stew in an iron pot. A fifth and sixth stood guard at points just beyond the light, hiding in the shadows of tall trees. The seventh stood in the center of the circle with a long staff, gazing off into the night.

Camber saw Tymon and Persa and witnessed the exchange of food and water. He felt a thrill when he saw that Persa was left untied. The feeling abated when he realized how far from the perimeter they were. Then he watched as the troll with the staff drew the circle around them. Preest warned them all about magic. Was this some magic cast to keep Tymon and Persa captive?

The night wore on. Fires faded to embers. Is bright night past, Camber wondered? Moon must still be strong above the clouds. He could see quite well in the dark under normal conditions. Tonight, he was able to discern many details around him.

During his vigil, Camber let his hands range about, gathering things that may prove useful. Little sharp sticks and stones of varying shapes and sizes were clustered within easy reach. Tymon and Persa had fallen asleep. So had most of the trolls. The two that guarded the camp were standing at a distance from him and looking away into the night. They remained quite still. If Camber had not known they were there, he may have mistaken them for large shrubbery.

He needed to get the attention of Persa and Tymon without alerting any of the trolls. Selecting several small pebbles, he took aim at Persa's sleeping form. One, then another and another arced through the night air in silence. The first struck her shoulder. She did not budge. The next two knocked against her head. She stirred a bit but did not awaken. Tymon raised his own head when Persa moved. He cast about the area with his one good eye.

Camber knew that Tymon probably could not see him, so he launched a small stone his direction. It plunked against Tymon's forehead. The boy ducked backward from the tiny impact, then raised himself higher, looking past Persa's sleeping form in the direction the pebble came from.

Camber risked being seen by rising up. Still crouched low, he raised one hand. On the offhand chance Tymon could see him, Camber flashed three fingers, then two. Tymon smiled and flashed two fingers back.

Immediately, the boy set about quietly rousing Persa. He pointed at Camber so Persa could find him in the dark. She smiled as well. If Camber was near, then her sister must be also! They would be saved from the trolls after all.

Slowly Tymon crouched, but he stopped moving whenever he got close to the circle drawn on the ground. He examined the circle and tentatively nudged one of the stones the troll placed around them. Immediately, the staff-wielding troll snorted and grunted and stirred in his sleep. Tymon looked out at Camber.

Camber was all for grabbing the two and running away as fast as they could. The problem was that, while Camber was very good in the dark, he did not think Persa was, and he knew that Tymon, with his wound, would have difficulty with depth perception. What if there were more trolls in the woods? What if Micha and Para were already captured by other trolls?

Doubt began to assail the boy. The thing about it was the trolls didn't seem to be threatening them at all. In fact, they took care of them for the most part. Maybe waiting was the right idea. If Micha were here, he would have a better plan.

So the three lay still, awake beneath a mythical mountain in the cloud-cast night. Close to day brightening, the troll with the staff arose and began working with some pouches and bowls. He mixed and poured and heated the compound over faded embers. He muttered what Camber thought to be incantations. After some time, while it was still dark, he walked over to where Tymon lay, carrying a small bowl.

He crossed the circle line and sat down on the ground in front of the boy. Both Persa and Tymon sat up at his approach and now were as far from him as they could get within the circle in the dirt. Camber gripped his knife and rose slightly, ready to spring.

The troll pointed at Tymon and then to the space in front of himself. "Here," he said. Pointing at Persa, then indicating his own eye, he said, "You. Help." The troll held up a bowl of weird smelling goo.

"Persa," Tymon said with attempted bravery, "I'm not going to swallow anything. So, if that's what he wants, don't help, alright?"

"No drink. Here." The troll seemed annoyed. He reached into the bowl and dabbed a bit of the mixture on his own face in the vicinity of his eye. Up close, Tymon could see a long scar on the troll's hairy face, diagonal across his own eye. "You hurt. This heal. You help." He again pointed at Persa. "No scream. Hurt." He tapped his own ear.

Tymon swallowed and edged forward. Gently, the troll tugged at the bandage about the boy's head. Persa jumped forward and pushed the troll's hand away. She undid the cloth. The troll made a surprised sound when he saw the wound. He whistled once, then several notes in a row. One of the other trolls whistled back.

"Torch," said the staff wielder. Camber was starting to think of him as the leader. The other troll grabbed a bundle of sticks and stirred them around in a firepit. Sparks flew up, and flames rose. The bundle caught fire and made a neat torch. The troll brought it over. He too made a surprised sound at the sight of Tymon's wounded eye.

Tymon stayed still despite the proximity of the flame. The troll with the staff leaned close, along with the torchbearer. Tymon and Persa could smell burning hair, and the trolls' faces smoked a little. Persa gasped in shock at Tymon's wound.

"Mmmph," the torch bearer grunted.

"Agree," said the staff wielder. "He need SHE."

Together, the two trolls looked up. Camber allowed his gaze to rise as well.

And there it was. Giant's Mountain. A dim shadow in the predawn gloom. They had been at the base all this time. The side of the mountain stretched straight up in a massive cliff face. The river valley below curved about the smooth walls. At the pinnacle of the sheer face, a soft golden light pulsed, stronger and brighter than when he first saw it the other night. Their trek this far had been a slight uphill climb. Back the way they had journeyed, the mountain sloped and tumbled like most other peaks. Only here at this side was it flat and long like a blade.

Camber lay on the forest floor and looked back at the tableau of trolls and children. The leader began to stroke a dark paste around Tymon's eye. The boy recoiled at first, then acquiesced. Persa cradled his head in her slim hands. When the paste had been applied, the troll indicated that Persa should wrap the bandage again. Then he said, "We bring you to SHE. SHE make magic for him. Maybe too late. Still we go to SHE. You come. Him too." And the troll pointed a hairy finger directly at Camber.

Camber was surprised. His surprise turned to terror at that moment. The woods erupted with screams and howls as men armed with crude spears and cudgels poured into the troll camp.

\*\*\*\*\*\*\*\*\*\*\*\*

"Camber will get them out, right, Micha? He can do that, rescue Persa and Tymon, right?" Para and Micha lay beneath a common blanket sharing warmth in the deep night. They could not risk a fire.

"We've been through this, Para. If he can do it without being seen he will, but I think he will wait for us to arrive. We may have to wait for a better opportunity. I just don't know, Para. Better to rest now and be ready when the time comes. Camber knows what he's doing. I trust him in this."

"You have trusted Camber longer than I have."

"You mean, I have trusted Camber, and you are just starting?"

"Yes." Para's voice was not quite contrite. "I never liked him much. He was always too rough with me. You remember, he would hold me down, pour dirt in my face or rub mud in my hair or push snow into my shirt. He just always touched me..." She paused for a moment. "He touched me wrong, Micha. Not like you." The girl pressed herself closer to the boy.

Micha had felt Para next to him before. Tonight was different. Her body was different, softer in some ways, longer maybe, and leaner than the tough little girl he watched growing up in the village streets. Micha's father had been friends with her father. Micha's father brought Para's father's body back from what they called the deadly hunt. Several men lost their lives or were severely wounded that time. What had been a hunt for one bear became a battle for survival when a pack of wolves, drawn by the scent of the bear's spilt blood, tracked them down at camp. The men won the battle, but only barely. Micha's father saved the day, or so the bard's song went. Micha's family then took on Para's family as their own.

Micha pulled the girl closer and stroked her hair. "I don't know how we will do it, Para, but we will get Persa and Tymon back."

"Tymon's ma must be scared about him. Yours and mine too. We've been gone a long time. Do you think they are looking for us?"

This thought plagued Micha. All his life he listened to the old stories. All his life he knew that parts were true and that some were only Preest's words to scare them into obedience. The night time drew Micha, not the same as it drew Camber, not from fear or the need for seeking sanctuary, but because the night was beautiful and soft. And it was wrong somehow. There should be more to the night than fear, he believed. More light in the dark. More sound in the silence.

When Micha saw the mountain, he felt drawn to it, and he knew he had to seek it out. There was truth there, and he needed to find it. The village was dying. He knew it once had been a town and that there were other towns too. Once, there were a great many people, and life was easy. Preest told him of Sun and summer and warmth and green fields. Preest had books. Micha knew them but did not know the words. He saw pictures and paintings, sketches from travelers. He saw books that Preest did not show other children. Micha's heart swelled in those times, but they were rare. Too many things took him away: wood and water, fire tending, leather tanning, roof thatching, skinning and sharpening, and all the myriad tasks necessary for the village's survival.

But he had seen the pictures. He saw what Preest showed him and knew there was something more. Once the village had been better, more alive. Once the world had been better. If only the giants would return, he had thought. Then, that one night, he slipped from the house and saw the mountain.

\*\*\*\*\*\*\*\*\*\*\*\*

Hunting was poor the last several months. Some in the village were sick, children and mothers. Three of the elders died. Summer, what there was of it, was soon ending. It never grew warm enough to plant much, and the rain kept the ground too wet. The cold kept the seeds dormant, and the harvest was non-existent. Gathering and gleaning would not provide through a harsh winter.

Preest did not want to leave the village, but the elders said that they must go south before winter set in. A dangerous, desperate proposition. South was where the Others were.

The first night he saw the mountain, it looked so close. Maybe, thought Micha, maybe I should go there and find the giants. Maybe they would teach us new ways to live through harsh days. Maybe they just forgot we are here. What could it hurt to try?

He did not expect Para and Persa to follow, and certainly not little Tymon. He should have turned back, but Para, scrappy, tough little Para, promised to tell his da that he was planning on leaving the village in search of Giant's Mountain. He had to let her tag along. Then Persa did the same thing, and then Tymon too. Well, at least he had gotten them to prepare for the journey. Water skins and blankets and provisions and slings and tinder and anything else they might need were gathered and distributed.

He had been on hunts. Most of them were uneventful and mundane. Micha truly believed that walking to Giant's Mountain would be simple. The bandit surprised them all. One solitary wanderer who tried to take without asking.

Poor Tymon found his courage defending Persa. Found his courage and lost his eye. Micha couldn't bring himself to say to the rest that Tymon's eye would never heal, but he saw it and knew that Camber did too.

Tymon defended Persa, and Micha saw the future for them in that action. Now he realized that he might be seeing the future for Para and himself. There would be a reckoning when they all returned to the village, and Micha knew he would be the one to pay the price. He would insist. That is, if the villagers were still there and had not begun the trek south.

\*\*\*\*\*\*\*\*\*\*\*\*

Para raised herself on one elbow, facing Micha. "Are they looking for us, Micha? Are we going to be in a lot of trouble? I'm sorry that I made you bring us all along, but I just couldn't stand the thought that you might leave the village and maybe never come back. If it had just been you and me, we would have been alright, right? You and me, we do good together, Micha. Don't you think so?"

Micha saw her face in the pale light of the not-quite-bright clouds. He saw her eyes shining at him, saw her hair fall around her cheeks and chin, saw her mouth, asking for assurances, but more. He let his arm tighten around her shoulders and drew her lips to his. Para sighed once and pressed against him, her arms circling his neck.

They kissed for a while as young people do, but soon the day's events pressed back into their tenderness. Para lay with her head cradled in Micha's shoulder. He said, "I am happy you are here. I trust you. I see who you are. I see who we are together, Para."

"You see who everybody is, Micha. You see Tymon for what he can be, and that makes him be that person. You see Camber for what he really is too, and he is not so bad, just in a bad house. Is it true? Did his da kill his ma? That would make anyone angry inside. I was mad at him for bringing the trolls to our camp, but he didn't do it, did he? We lit the fire and that's how the trolls found us, right?"

"They are not trolls. I remember the stories Preest made up about trolls. These ones, they are not bad. They are dwarves. I learned from Preest's books. They are ancient, Para. They come from the days of dragons and giants. They know where Giant's Mountain is, and I think they are going there now."

"Then why did they take Persa and Tymon?"

"I don't know. We have to follow them and see."

Para sat up and threw off the blanket. The cold night air struck Micha's chest and made him gasp. "Did you tell Camber to leave them with the trolls so you could find Giant's Mountain?"

"No! I wouldn't do that!"

"Because if you did, Micha, if we could have gotten them away and didn't because of your silly quest, I will punch you so hard!"

"I didn't, alright?" Micha sat up and spoke in soothing tones. "I didn't, and I wouldn't, and keep your voice down. And they are dwarves, not trolls."

Para sat back, arms and legs crossed.

"Look…" Micha sought to placate Para's changed mood. "Why don't we roll up camp and try to find Camber. If we can get them away, we will. If not, at least we're all together. Sort of. I don't know if the village is searching for us, but they probably aren't searching this far, not yet at least. If we can get Persa and Tymon away, we'll go back. Giant's Mountain has been there all these years. It will be there longer. I can always find it later."

Para leaned forward and said, "We. We can always find it later."

Micha smiled and started to roll up camp. There was not much to gather, and no fire meant no cleanup. Together they slipped off into the pale night, hand in hand, with Para in the lead.

# 4
# RAGE AND RESCUE

THOUGHTS POURED INTO CAMBER IN A RUSH. Not thoughts really, but actions. Decisions were not being made with any consciousness.

Filthy, yellow-eyed men leapt out of the dying night, scrabbling past Camber, who was still hidden, still covered with leaves. They did not notice the boy. They came from all about, screaming fiercely. Each one carrying short spears of wood and stone. Each one seeking a target.

The trolls also leapt into action, cudgels and knives appearing in their hands. They sought to take positions, a vee shape first, but in the initial chaos, they ended up back-to-back. The two trolls guarding the perimeter burst from where they were hiding and dove into the fray, breaking the momentum of the assault. For a moment, Camber believed the attackers might flee. But there were so many, and Camber could hear more approaching.

Camber's first impression was that the men of the village had found them and were rescuing the children. But the men of the village were stealthy and cautious. They were also well-equipped and disciplined in their attacks. His own father drilled them to precision and was the one who generally led the hunt. That thought brought a sense of reality to Camber as he recalled the lifeless form he had run from. It froze him for a moment.

No, the attackers were not of his village. He now recognized descriptions given by elders of the Others across the river. Dressed in filthy, rough hides, with matted hair, sallow skin, and faces and arms smeared with ochre and umber, they bore crude spears with chipped stone tips. The trolls were hard-pressed to defend themselves against the savage horde.

Two of the Others swept forward toward Persa and Tymon, raising their short spears. Persa cowered, eyes wide. Tymon stood in front of Persa, brandishing his little knife.

Camber could see the future, but he could not change it. No matter how fast he moved, the Other's spear would finish the bandit's work and take Tymon to the Grey Lord's kingdom.

Then, one of the trolls broke ranks, hurling himself toward the children. Skidding to a stop in front of Tymon and Persa, whirling his cudgel and axe, stepping forward to strike in defense of the children, the shaggy troll growled low. The attackers fell back at his ferocity. Camber felt the echo of the troll's growl deep in his own chest.

Seizing the chance, rising from his hiding place, Camber armed his sling, hurling by instinct one of the larger stones. The missile flew to its target, felling the leader of the attack against the children. As he dropped, the second man, thrusting his spear wildly from behind his fellow, inflicted a deep grazing wound in the troll's right thigh.

Darting around the wounded troll, Tymon returned the wound by plunging his knife into the thigh of the Other, causing considerably more damage. Screaming, the man dropped to one knee. The troll's cudgel swung. Tymon heard him say, "No screamin'!" Two attackers were down. The small clearing remained in chaos.

Camber slung three more stones. Each unerring. Each deadly. In his chest he felt a rage rising. His eyesight swam. His vision narrowing. His voice altered, lowering, and turning to a deep growl. His hearing focused and brought his attention to the ravening horde of bedraggled attackers. His intensified sight brought him information from the poorly lit troll camp. The scent of the invaders, rank and angry, filled his nostrils.

All seven of the trolls now surrounded Persa and Tymon, shielding the children with their own bodies. Every troll suffered a handful of wounds.

Camber could smell blood. He saw the number of attackers already dispatched lying lifeless on the ground. He could sense the difference between the blood of the Others and the blood of the trolls.

The clouds broke. Low in the sky, just above the treetops, Moon shone down on them all. Unfiltered and clear, pale light bathed the scene of battle. Camber erupted in fury. Leaping into the troll camp, his knife in one hand, he gathered a fallen short spear in the other. Whirling, stabbing, slicing, Camber wreaked havoc on the attacking horde.

The Others sought to rally, to bring the boy down by strength of numbers. He was too fast, his actions too savage, the power of his fury too intense. Like a storm shredding a forest, Camber launched himself from one enemy to another until they all began to fall away.

\*\*\*\*\*\*\*\*\*\*\*\*

Micha and Para arrived at the top of a ridge just as the attack began. They did not fully comprehend all that was occurring but witnessed the dwarf saving Persa and Tymon. They saw Camber alter and change. They saw his ferocious attack. Together they hurled themselves down the path, emerging to find the battle nearly ended.

Camber, bloodied and panting, stood wild-eyed and growling. Bodies lay around him, some still, many twitching their final spasms of life. The dwarves closed ranks between the bestial boy and his terrified friends.

Camber only knew that they were in his way of rescuing his companions. He started to prowl forward, clutching his bloody knife. The dwarves spread out, keeping up a constant whistling communication. The high pitch of the sound seemed to irritate Camber.

Micha and Para tumbled out of the forest at this point. Two dwarves turned to face what they perceived as a potentially new menace. When they saw Micha and Para, they returned their attention to the threat facing their fellows.

Camber threw his head back and let loose a howl. He charged across the camp.

Stepping into the space between Persa, Tymon, and their defenders, Micha braced himself to take the brunt of Camber's rage-driven charge.

Para sped up, darting past Micha. She met Camber halfway. Surprised, he pulled up and skid to a halt a few paces away from the girl. She did the same, spreading her arms and opening her hands.

"Camber! It's me, Para! Micha too! We are here with you. You did it! You saved us, Camber! You saved Persa and Tymon. Camber. Look at me. Look, it's me, Para. From our village. Your friend, Camber! Your friend Para. Look!"

Camber growled still, pacing to and fro, looking first at the ones between him and his friends, then at this girl, who once hated him and now was professing friendship. He sliced his bloody knife through the air and jabbed the spear at the sky. Para kept on.

"Camber, look at me. Just look." Her voice lowered in tone, and she swayed in front of him seeking to remain in his sight. "Camber, you're alright. Camber, you're *not* a beast. You are a man. Please look at me! We are your friends, Camber. And the trolls are not trolls. Just like Micha told us, no trolls. They are dwarves, Camber, and they know where Giant's Mountain is. We saw it, Camber. You saw it too. They can show us the way! Camber, stop! Look. Look at me." Camber slowed and ceased growling. His steps grew shorter, and he focused on Para's face.

"I'm sorry, Camber. For all the times I didn't understand you. You hurt me sometimes. You made me afraid sometimes. I'm afraid now, but you are my friend,

Camber. You are our friend. Come back to us. Stop fighting. All the Others have run away. You saved the dwarves. You saved Persa and Tymon. Look, Camber. Look at me."

And he did look. His eyes cleared. His heaving breath altered. The boy began to sob. Camber fell to his knees weeping. "I killed them! I couldn't stop! They were going to kill Tymon. I couldn't let that happen! I killed them all. I killed him too. I killed my father before he could kill me. I killed him! Now I am like him." He spoke low and soft. Only Para heard his words clearly.

Tymon came up behind Para. Circling around her he knelt down with the weeping boy, hugging him while Para made soft words. Micha too approached, laying a hand on Camber's head. Persa came up next to Para and held her sister's hand in silence. Moon disappeared from sight behind the treeline as clouds returned to cover the sky.

\*\*\*\*\*\*\*\*\*\*\*\*

Daylight found them this way. At the base of Giant's Mountain, the sun they had never seen rose on the far side, still hidden, but not by clouds. Together, dwarves and children, recovered in the shadow of an ancient time.

The dwarves kept busy dragging the bodies of the Others away into the woods and straightening their camp. The river was not far away. They washed Camber's face, hands, and arms the best they could with the water they carried. They bound their own wounds with rough cloth.

Camber slept.

Later in the day, one of the dwarves came back into camp bearing full skins of water. In silence, he gathered wood and materials to cook. The children awoke from napping, all except Camber.

They thanked the dwarves for taking care of Tymon. His eye was free from pain.

The staff wielder said, "No pain good. Not good enough. We taking he to SHE in the mountain. Soon enough, SHE might save boy's eye. Saved mine." He pointed to his own hairy face. Beneath the hair they could observe a scar similar to Tymon's own wound. "Fear we too late for boy. Sick get inside eye. SHE make clean. He live. One eye. We go. You go too."

"Go where?" Micha asked. The dwarf pointed at the side of the cliff and said no more. They were taciturn and quiet much of the day, a few whistles back and forth, but not much speech. They stayed on guard as the children fell back into exhausted slumbers. Micha remained awake for a time staring at his little band, feeling bad about getting them into such trouble. At one point he approached the leader and asked, "Can you help us get back to our village?"

The leader scratched at his face, looked at the mountain and said, "We help you go to the mountain top." He turned and walked away from Micha, saying, "Sleep now. We go tonight."

Micha spent a few moments covering the others with their bedding, then lay down next to Para. He looked up at the sky. He had seen Moon. It was a real thing, just like Preest said. Hearing the howling and the din of the battle beginning, he and Para broke cover and raced to the clear area near the dwarves' camp. The night lit up as the clouds broke. Micha looked up into the sky, and when he looked down, Para was already racing to the fight. He was hard pressed to catch up. In the fury and aftermath of the battle, there was little time to consider what he witnessed in the sky.

As he lay on his back, he knew his life was altered in ways too deep to comprehend. The very sky itself would never be the same. The clouds were thick and heavy as always, but today they were different. Patches of blue shone through, and sometimes the edges of the clouds were a bright white. The shadow of the mountain covered them, and the day remained cool. Despite being a long way from home, lost and wounded, Micha fell asleep thinking that the world looked brighter.

The scent of food woke Micha. Sometime during his sleep Para curled into his arms. Persa and Tymon curled up together as well, but Micha knew this was different. He brushed his fingers against Para's cheek and forehead. When her eyes fluttered open, he leaned close and kissed her lips gently. The girl smiled and stretched. Together they roused Persa and Tymon but allowed Camber to remain asleep. Clouds covered the sky again, and the world took on the familiar muted tones. Micha thought about telling them what he saw, about the sky, but did not feel he had the words for it.

The dwarves passed around spoons, and bowls filled with hot stew, and the four youths sat and shared the meal in grateful silence. After they were sated, the dwarves and the human children began breaking camp. Micha went to Camber, and from a slight distance called to him, singing an old song and chanting his name in low tones.

Camber stirred slowly. He blinked several times and said dreamily, "Ma, Mama, I am here." The boy stirred and stretched. Opening his eyes fully he saw Micha and said, "Micha, I thought...I must have been dreaming, but it is all true, is it not? We were fighting. I was..."

"There was a great battle, Camber. You were magnificent. Pretty scary too. You are a battlecrafter for certain. You and Tymon, both before me. Are you hurt?"

"I am sore, but I think I'm alright." Tears welled in his eyes. "I cannot go back, Micha. I can never go back to the village. My da, he..." Tears streamed. "He tried to kill me, Micha, like he killed ma. I saw that, Micha, long ago. Did I...?" Camber reached for Micha and clutched his sleeve. "Did I turn...into...some beast? My da, he would turn, and I would run, and you were the only one who knew, Micha. Now they know too, don't they?" Camber looked at Para, Persa, and Tymon. "Did I hurt them, Micha? Did I try and hurt them? Is Tymon afraid of me now? What will I do, Micha? What can I do?"

"The dwarves say we will go to the mountain top. They say tonight. I don't know what they are talking about really. They actually don't talk much at all, mostly whistle. I think we should just follow them, Camber. We've come this far, and everything is different now. I saw Moon. I might have seen Sun too, but for the mountain."

Micha reached out and held Camber by his arms. They leaned close to each other and stared into each other's eyes. "Camber, we are a little scared. About you, I mean. But we are not afraid of you. You saved them, Camber. You saved Tymon and Persa, and they know it. I don't know if you turned into something else. I mean, what would do that? But you were pretty fierce and scary. We are in this together, Camber, you and me and the others. Let's try and figure it out together." The boys leaned forward, pressing their foreheads together.

Para appeared with some stew and water. She handed both to Camber and then sat next to Micha.

"You called me 'friend,' Para," Camber said. "I remember that. I know you only said so to calm me down, but I liked hearing it. I won't hold you to anything you said."

"If not friends, then at least we are companions," Para replied. "We have been through a lot in a few days, Camber. I think you will go through a lot more. I heard Micha and I agree. Let us try and figure this out together."

"Companions." Camber tried the word aloud. "That is a good word. Para, I won't pretend about the past, and I can't promise about the future, but right now, I am sorry about everything I ever did or said that made you afraid."

Para was quiet. She sat still, watching Camber eat the stew. Finally, she said, "Right now is enough."

One of the dwarves approached. "Get ready. Soon we go."

Para went to Persa and Tymon and helped them gather their gear. Micha and Camber pulled their packs together as well, sharpening their blades and then those of the rest of the band.

Para handed her blade to Micha and said, "I expect that you will hand me your knife someday soon." Micha smiled at this, thinking on the handfasting ceremonies he had seen in the village, one partner pledging their strength and power to the other, symbolized by the cording of the wrists and the trading of knives. A year and a day, he thought while looking into Para's grey eyes. They already knew each other all their lives. In front of Camber and Persa and Tymon, without a word Micha took Para's wrist in his hand. She gripped his wrist in return, and he handed his knife to her.

"Whatever the future, we are together," Micha said.

"A year and a day," Para replied. The other children gathered around them and hugged the couple tightly. Even Camber got in on the scene and everyone, in turn, hugged him as well.

The dwarves stood near. The sky darkened. The leader read from rune markings on his staff. The children did not understand the language, but each felt the power of ancient knowledge. His companions whistled notes, sometimes in chorus and other times in harmonies. The cliff wall echoed back their song, and sound filled the valley like freshening winds.

The ground shuddered. Rocks and dust cascaded off the cliff. A crack appeared in the stone. Long and straight, from the ground up at least three times the height of the dwarves. In the waning light of day, the mountain opened. The dwarves stepped inside the tall portal. Each rummaged about to the sides of a dark chamber and came up with long sticks. A scrape of flint brought sparks and then flame to the sticks, turning them into torches. They beckoned the children to enter.

"We all saw Giant's Mountain," said Micha. "We all said we wanted to see it close. We all said we wanted to leave the village to seek answers. I say we got what we asked for and more. I have more questions now than before. I believe the answers lie ahead. Are we all still together?" They all replied yes. All save Camber.

Para turned and walked to him, asking, "Camber, are you coming?"

"I didn't see what you did when you did. I am only here because I needed to escape the village. You yourself said I wasn't one of you. I will enter the mountain with you, but I enter it alone."

"You enter it with us because you are *with* us. You are not alone." Para held out her hand to Camber.

The boy was grateful for the darkness. His tears were hidden. He took Para's hand, and she led him to the head of their group. The dwarves handed them each a torch and trudged forward into a cavernous entrance.

"Companions," Para said, leading the other four into the mountain, Camber behind her, followed by Tymon and Persa, then Micha watching their backs.

# 5

# THE LONG DARK

ONCE INSIDE, THEY GAZED IN WONDER at the carved rock. Spiral columns, statues of fantastic creatures and beings, doorways and halls stretching off differing directions, the ceiling lost in darkness where the torchlight could not reach. Stairs were carved into the cavern wall. The dwarves led the way upwards.

The companions followed them, first up the side of the cavern and then into smooth, curved tunnels. Sometimes they walked through narrow, cylindrical halls, barely large enough for the dwarves. Other times they found themselves traversing massive stone bridges over valleys of pitch-black depths. They had no notion of passing time or how long they had been climbing.

Several times, they paused with the dwarves for water and bread. Low conversation was begun, but their words echoed and amplified through the caves. In the distance, they could hear tumbling stones and popping cracks, each sound accenting their echoing words. The dwarves, eyes wide and all at once, put fingers to their lips to indicate silence. One, dressed in a floppy hat, leaned in and whispered, "No talk. Walls fall." From that point, there was silence amongst them.

Little whistles came from the dwarves, accompanied by clicks and hums. Micha realized that they were speaking a private language. Low tones kept the walls from collapsing.

They came to a small room with carved benches and nooks in the walls. Here the dwarves set down their gear. Again, speaking in low tones, the one with the floppy hat said, "Find nook. Make bed. We rest. We sleep. We go. No talk."

Cold dried meats, bread, and nuts made a satisfying meal. The group soon fell asleep. Micha and Para shared one nook, while Camber lay in front of another, guarding Tymon and Persa as they slept together for warmth. Micha heard Persa softly cry herself to sleep. At varying moments during the sleeping period, Micha woke and saw one or another of the dwarves sitting quietly with a lit torch casting a pool of warm light around him. That one always faced Camber.

When they woke they set about securing their gear. After re-igniting all the torches, the band of travelers set out. They climbed for some time before they arrived at what first looked like a wooden-walled room. The dwarves entered without hesitation, beckoning the companions to follow. All torches save four were extinguished. Those four were secured in iron mounts at the corners of the room.

"Is this place shaking?" Para asked Micha in very quiet tones. Together they looked at the place where the stone tunnel led into the wooden room. As the band moved about, stowing gear against the three walls, the floor swayed to and fro, closer then farther from the cavern floor, a handspan, maybe more.

Persa and Tymon stood in the center, eyes wide and arms around each other. Camber pushed their packs into the corners evenly, as directed by two of the dwarves. The leader pointed and whistled, and slowly a fourth wall descended, sealing them off from the mountain cavern. He once again consulted his staff, though this time he did not speak. As the fourth wall touched the floor, panels on either side of the room opened, revealing wooden levers inside. Micha watched closely as they were pulled, first one, then another, a complex but precise pattern.

A slight jolt sent Para into Micha's arms. Persa squeaked, then whimpered, gripping Tymon's jerkin. Camber swung protective, steadying arms around the two. The room began to quiver, and they could see through cracks and gaps in the wood that the rock walls were moving.

"Sit," the leader said with a smile. "Go up easy! Giant's way! Way of King." Micha then realized that the room itself was rising.

\*\*\*\*\*\*\*\*\*\*\*\*

Outside the caverns, the young villagers knew day from night, despite the fact that Sun and Moon were hidden from their sight by constant clouds. Inside the mountain, with only torchlight all the time, every moment felt the same. Time passed, but how much? Hours may have passed, or days. The motion of the rising room lulled them, but was it time to sleep?

The dwarves pulled out some sticks, unwrapping them from their leather ties. The companions could see they were of varying sizes, some the length of a finger, some the length of a hand or foot. Each dwarf pulled a pouch off his belt or out of a pocket, dumping the contents onto the floor. Brilliant gems sparkled beneath the torchlight. They began a game, the rules of which were incomprehensible to the human youth.

Camber watched the dwarves for a while, then lay down and slept. Eventually Tymon did the same. Persa sat in the center of the room whimpering until Para and Micha beckoned her over to them. They wrapped arms around her and pulled their cloaks together, covering her head. Persa fell into a fitful slumber, twitching and whimpering until Para lay down next to her sister.

Micha caught the eye of the leader. "Why us?" he asked quietly. The room rose, occasionally squeaking or bumping, making loud noises that echoed above and below them. He felt he could chance some speech. The leader looked at him for a bit, then came and sat nearby.

"You scared?" the leader asked Micha.

"Yes, actually I am. Why are you helping us? Or are you? Are we your captives?"

"You scared." He nodded. "Good. SHE is scary." He pointed upwards. "Come back to her father's castle SHE did. Angry. Feels life unfair SHE does. Us, we watch your village. Once her father built things. Your village is the last.

King still happy then. Ah! Longtimes. Many human lifetimes. We still talk to Preest. He is a Keeper. When you leave, he calls We. Asks We to find you. We find you. Preest no say, 'Bring them back!' HaHa!"

The dwarf spoke freely, and Micha remained quiet. "You do good in wood. You speak nice to forest. We think SHE will like to see why We stay and keep watch. So," he shrugged and raised his hands upwards, "you come with We, and We see SHE."

"Who is SHE?" Micha emphasized the word as a title just as the dwarf did.

"You will see SHE! Soon too." The dwarf leaned in and spoke quieter. "You free. Always it was with the father, the King. He wish for humans to be better. SHE wants to be the King's daughter again, only, no King! No King, no Princess."

"The giant? He was a King?"

"He was THE King! Only he gone away." The dwarf sounded sad.

"Preest tells many tales, but not this one. When did he go? Where is he?"

"When? Long ago. Before you and all that Preest remembers. King Kane his name. Once he walked with dragons. When dragons there were. You know dragons? I *know* dragons. Where King is now? In the ground. He is planted, and when the season is good, he will grow again."

Micha's eyes narrowed. He heard this kind of fable before. Some great being would return to save all the people in the future. Many wanted to believe this and failed to work for themselves. Many looked forward for succor. They stopped living for the present day and dreamt of rescue from hard work. Micha believed this was why the village was failing. Micha knew that a good hunt today meant food and clothing tomorrow. A good gather meant warmth and shelter. He waited for no one to rescue him.

"You not believe? No? It is truth. Only…" The dwarf shrugged in resignation. "Maybe he never grow. Or maybe it is far away in years. No matter. We dig. You plant. You hunt. Life is life, and Gaia is good."

"What do you mean Preest is a Keeper? What does he keep?"

"Words. Knowings. He know much but says what is needed. He knows SHE. Only long time past." The dwarf pondered Micha for a moment. "You are not knowing. You are not told about the…before."

"Before what? I feel like I know nothing."

"You know something. Hehe." The dwarf stroked his beard. "You see the mountain. No one sees the mountain but those who know. Dragons' blood. That what you know. It calls you. You answer."

"I do not understand."

"No. You are not in the head understanding, but in your blood, you know a truth. You went to mountain. The mountain that isn't there! That what Preest say, yes? That what everybody say? Everybody say, 'No mountain. No giant.' But everybody know mountain and Giant King story. Why say no when is yes? Confusing. But you know! You see, and you know something. So now you see more, and you know more. Soon you know more than what you know now! HaHaHA! Soon see much. Soon see SHE! Soon see world. Feel small. Haha."

Micha was feeling more confused than ever, and the dwarf wasn't helping him. He decided to change subjects. "Who are you? What do the markings on your staff mean? What do you do for…SHE?"

"Do? We dig! Stones and gems. Pretty things for SHE, yes?" He reached into a pocket and pulled out a handful of sparkling stones. Micha had seen their like before when the dwarves were playing their stick game. Up close, the playing stones were pretty enough. The ones he saw now were captivating. He heard of such things, but in his village there was little time for such distraction. Weapons and cook fires, catching and skinning, chopping and building, these were the things that occupied the villagers' lives. Carved wood, some pipes or stretched string across hollow wood, some feathers or bone made up the arts that they experienced. Holding these jewels in his hands, Micha sat mesmerized, gazing at the flashing light that seemed to emanate from within the gems. Deep red, a green he had never seen, golden yellow, and some clear as ice rolled about in the hairy hand of the leader.

"We once trade with the King." The dwarf's mood shifted again. Eyes unfocused, he looked down and then up as if seeing a far different time. We happy to trade with SHE, but is different. SHE seeks beauty. King sought quality. King make beauty from stones. SHE make piles of stones. We trade. Little in return. Enough.

"We live below. Below mountain. Below valley. Below village. Safe there. Staff carries runes. I carry staff.

Is ancient messages. I received. I pass down to next one, next leader. Maybe you want a staff? Hahe. You lead good!"

"Me? I didn't. Tymon lost his eye. We almost lost him and Persa to you. Then the Others attacked. They must have been tracking us, and I didn't even suspect. We could have all died. Some leader I am." Micha could hear the morose sound of his voice and felt the rising swell of self-pity.

"Lost boy and girl to We? Not! We take them to SHE. You followed good. Boy brave. We not knowing about you before. Preest ask We to find you, but you not easy to find. Good leader! You get help from forest. You make decision." He nodded to the other companions and said, "They do for you. Good leader! You make fire. We find you. Eh, not so smart that. They come too, ones you call Others. Just humans. Scared humans. Always scared…humans. We try to guide you to mountain. Others, they fast. You hide other boy, scary boy, near us. We never know! Haha! Good leader! He fast, scary. Scary as SHE! Nasty humans, they die. Now they fear. They always fear. They fear You now! Good leader!" The dwarf leader laughed and twinkled as he spoke. His hands and arms jerked about as he described his version of events. He clapped Micha on the shoulder. "Good leader like me!"

Micha laughed. "I guess so. Do you have a name? I am called Micha."

The dwarf thought a bit. "I am…" and he whistled a short tune. "You are…" and he whistled three notes, then two, the same signal Micha gave to Camber and the others.

The dwarf smiled as Micha laughed. "SHE call me Docha. Micha and Docha, eh? Cha, cha. Hehehehe. So we brothers? HAha! Maybe!"

Micha found himself relaxing and laughing now. How much time passed since they entered the moving room he did not know. It was turning into pleasant time though. He liked Docha.

"Brothers and friends?" Micha said.

"We all friends!" Docha said, laughing loudly. Para stirred, opening a sleepy, wary eye.

Micha stroked her hair away from her face. "We all friends," he said to her, smiling.

"That is good to know," Para said. "I can stop planning to escape then?"

Micha laughed. "Yes. I believe we are safe now. Except of course for SHE!" He and Docha laughed.

"SHE may keep you! You all good. Good enough for SHE!"

"Unless we escape," said Para.

The remainder of the ride in the moving room was spent sharing food and drink and introductions. The dwarves loved little Tymon and wanted to hear his triumph over the bandit again and again. Tymon spun the tale a little differently each time. The dwarves called out suggestions and modifications to make the stories more dramatic.

Tymon leaned over to Camber and whispered, "This isn't really how it happened! I really just sort of tripped, and I only wanted to stop him from hurting Persa and…"

Camber laughed and said, "Well, all those big tales told after the long hunts aren't really how it happened either. We tell the story this way to encourage others. You are a hero now. Maybe we can write a song about you?"

Tymon blushed but smiled. "I am no hero."

"Well you look like one to me." Camber tugged Tymon's bandage tighter, brushing at the boy's hair, knotted and matted with his own blood. "Battlecrafter's badge!"

"You are a hero, Camber," Tymon said. "You saved us all. Wait until your da and the village hear about that!" Camber grew silent and still. Micha heard the exchange but kept quiet. He sat with an arm around Para's shoulders.

All the while they traveled upward in the rising room. No matter what tasks or games went on, Micha noted that at least one of the dwarves was constantly watching Camber.

\*\*\*\*\*\*\*\*\*\*\*\*

The room began to slow. Vibrations changed, and the rhythmic shuddering intensified for a few moments, then began to lessen as they came to a gentle halt. The wall opposite the original entrance rose. They walked out into a large, stone hallway. Granite blocks were configured as support for the walls and roof. The dwarves took unlit torches and, touching them to the flames of the still burning corner lights, passed one to Camber and one to Micha. One of the dwarves, Udamon by name, took a flaming branch and led the way, smiling. The others fell in line behind him with Docha and the companions following.

The passage was large and long, and the group walked for some unknown time. "It is hard to walk," Persa said. "I don't know where I am." Her voice told her fear.

"It's alright," Micha said. "We must be close now."

"I'm here, Persa." Tymon reached out to take her hand.

"Girl tunnel-sick. No night, no day, makes her sleepy at the wrong times. We see Sun soon. Stairs ahead. We carry girl, only…No kicking!" Docha laughed and slapped Kyniko, who rubbed at his hairy chin and let a low noise trail from his throat.

True to his word, the stairway appeared after a short walk. Kyniko eyed Persa warily and then knelt in front of her. With his thick, hairy thumb he indicated she climb onto his broad back. Persa hesitated a moment then did just so, tucking her knees into his bent arms as he clasped his hands behind his back. As she slid her arms about his thick neck she whispered, "I'm sorry I kicked you. I was afraid."

Kyniko growled a reply. "No afraid of me, girl. Keep you safe before. Keep you safe now." Persa hugged him tight around the neck until he said, "Girl! Like me less, choke me less." Together they started up the stairs. Tymon approached the stairway and sighed. Camber was close. "You going to make it, hero?"

"I don't know. Maybe I should rest."

"Maybe. Here." Setting his torch on the cavern floor, Camber shifted his pack around to hang in front and knelt in the same manner as Kyniko did. "Rest on my back a while." Tymon hesitated a second, looking at Micha, who nodded yes. The boy clambered up on Camber's back.

Micha turned to look at Para. Before he could speak, she said, "Don't expect me to carry you, Micha!" And she started up the stairs on her own.

Docha came up behind Micha. "Fast tongue. Sharp words. Could be my daughter's secret sister. HaHA!" He stepped quick to follow Para.

Micha and a dwarf called Boleslau brought up the rear. As they passed Camber's torch Boleslau extinguished it against the stone wall. "No need bright. Enough with one." He nodded at Micha and held his empty hand high. Micha followed his example and raised the torch upward. There was plenty of room between the flame and the ceiling.

Ahead Tymon whispered to Camber, "I thought everything would be bigger." The hallway and the stairs were wide and tall, but not so different than the great hall of the village.

"I know what you mean, Tymon. It doesn't seem big enough for a giant. Not the ones in Preest's stories."

"HoHO! You thinking you know what a giant's castle like? You listen too much to Preest. He not know; he pretend to know. Should know. Preest forget. Preest tells good stories. Giants not so big, just giant. They big inside. You see soon. More steps for one hundred breaths. My breaths...maybe for you two hundred. Then we knock on the door."

************

The torches were smoky and the passage dank. Camber was breathing heavily, and Tymon was just about to volunteer to walk a while when, out of the thick black shadows at the end of the passage, a massive panel of wood, bound with iron, appeared in the torchlight.

"Find door. Now we knock," Docha said, motioning for Micha to follow him. They made for the front of the band of travelers. Udamon stood close to the massive door. He was holding a guttering torch, nearly spent. Micha's too, was wavering, like a flame in the breeze. But the air inside the cavern was still, and the smoke gathered in an alcove by the iron-hinged wooden panel.

Docha gazed at his staff. With a whistle he indicated Udamon and Micha should hold their torches aloft, casting a wider pool of firelight. Docha began walking to and fro close to the door, directing Myshkin to rap with his cudgel at various points and varying times. Sometimes the door boomed in response. Other times it sounded thick and flat. After a bit, the two dwarves stopped their strange actions and stood back, waiting.

Para came and stood close to Micha. He counted breaths. After two hundred, a large cracking noise sounded from above them. The children jumped at the sound. Persa tightened her arms again around Kyniko's neck. He said, "No fear, girl. No fear, childrens. Door opens."

Docha laughed. "Fear then! HoHO!"

The other dwarves laughed, except Kyniko and Myshkin. Micha heard Myshkin say quietly, "No scary to me. Pretty to me."

The wooden portal groaned and protested its own motion. Booming echoes caromed to and fro in the chamber before the door. Thunderous pounding made them all cover their ears. The door swung wide, and the sound tapered off to a rhythmic rattle.

"Oh HO! Well, SHE knows we are here now!" Docha flung his arms wide and uttered words that the children could not comprehend.

Para clung to Micha's arm. "Is that magic? Preest warned us about magic."

Micha patted her arm. "We are far beyond Preest's tales, Para. Don't worry. We'll be alright."

"I am not worried!" Para snapped at Micha but did not let go.

Pale light filtered through the widening opening. The light appeared bright and intense. Everyone held their hands up to their eyes. Fresh, cold air swept into the tunnel. The stale, dank smell vanished in a stiff breeze.

Docha turned to face them all. "No talking to SHE. If SHE wants talk from you, SHE will ask for your words. Until then, no talking to SHE." He turned and faced the opened door, then turned back to the travelers. "Except me. No talking to SHE except me." And he turned and led them all into a vast marbled hallway.

Again, Micha heard Myshkin speaking softly, almost to himself, saying, "She talk me."

Kyniko let Persa slip away to the floor and helped her gather her cloak about her shoulders. The air was wintery, and the wind cut through Persa and Tymon's rough cloth jerkins and breeches. Micha, Para, and Camber all slung their own cloaks about them while Docha and the others looked on.

# 6

# THE COLD LIGHT OF SHE

THE SEVEN SET A PACE, and the five companions followed easily. The hallway arched high above them and stretched far ahead. As far as they could see, beams of light cast from doorways on the right, fading to shadow on the left.

They were used to walking rough forest floors or the uneven tunnels of the mountain. This floor was perfectly flat and, though dusty, the polish gleamed in slanting rays of light. Sunlight, Micha realized. Unfiltered by clouds.

As they walked, they passed vast rooms and grand staircases. To their left, the rooms all appeared empty, shadowed. Within the depths, they caught glimpses of deep red curtains and white marble walls with hints of gold sparkling from corners and ceilings. To the right, bare rooms ended in massive windows through which the companions could see cloudless blue sky. Drifts of snow covered much of the floor in these rooms. The surface sparkled in the high light of the mountain sun.

"Rooms full of winter," Micha said to Para.

"I wonder if there are rooms full of summer," she replied.

Their eyes squinted nearly shut from the brightness. Daylight in the village was never this bright, and they had just spent an indeterminate amount of time in the dark of the caverns. Leaning forward, the dwarves let their hair fall across forehead and temple, granting them shadowed eyes.

Para noted Camber stumble, his arm across his brow to shield his eyes. She paused mid-step until he caught up with her. Reaching up, she pulled Camber's cloak forward and over his head, repeating the action for Persa and Tymon. The three bowed their heads, letting the loose folds of cloth shelter their faces from the light. Micha noted Para's action, and together they pulled their hoods upward as well, but neither bowed down. Unspoken, Para let her gaze roam to the shadowy left, while Micha took the view to the brilliant right. They hung back a few paces, with Tymon, Persa, and Camber just ahead and between them.

Keeping one hand clasped upon the hilt of her knife, Para maintained one diligent eye on her sister, Tymon, and Camber, while warily scanning darkened openings they passed. Persa began to whimper, walking with her eyes downcast and saying softly, "Why is there no dirt? Why are there no trees?" Soon Kyniko positioned himself directly behind the girl.

They walked a while longer, Micha counting breaths, but always losing focus as they passed magnificent archways and broad halls. He endured the brightness for the richness of the visions he was witnessing. Never, not in any of Preest's pictures, had he seen such sights. There was little true comprehension, only awe.

\*\*\*\*\*\*\*\*\*\*\*\*

The party finally arrived at a high, pointed portal at the end of the long hall. Great ornate doors hung open. They passed through in silence. Entering a massive circular room, they could see distant mountain peaks through wide arched windows that ringed most of the perimeter walls. Inside this room, Micha counted thirteen white pillars. Six to the left of the doorway and also to the right, reaching from floor to ceiling, supporting a domed roof. The last was on a dais directly ahead of the troupe. It rose not near as high as the ceiling and, Micha noted, it was not serving any apparent purpose. It was whiter than the others and more slender.

Docha quickened his steps while the troupe slowed. The companions followed suit, coming to a stop behind the six remaining dwarves. Micha watched Docha walk to the thirteenth pillar. The boy's eyes widened as the pillar began to shimmer and flow. Slowly, the pillar turned around. Micha saw it was no pillar at all.

In front of them stood SHE.

Docha fell to his knees and the other dwarves followed his lead. Para looked to Micha. He nodded and signaled they should do the same. All the members of the troupe knelt. Except one.

Tymon stood staring, his one good eye focused on the being who coalesced in front of him. Never before had such a sight greeted him. Tymon's world was small, and the women of the village were rugged and fit for survival. There was little art in his life, and no depiction ever presented such a being as now stood before him. Though he was a boy, somewhere within was the seed of a man. In this very moment, that seed sprouted.

All that occurred since the leaving of his village: the bandit and Tymon's death dealing, waking bound with Persa in what they thought was a troll camp, the attack by the Others and his own participation in defending the trolls, Camber's shapeshifting, the journey into the mountain, all these things stripped away his perceptions of the world, eroding his reality. Prior to leaving on this journey, much of what Tymon believed about the world outside the village walls was frightening. He could always imagine fear. Here appeared beauty truer than any he could ever imagine. Tymon's heart swelled with gratitude at the sight of her.

A shimmering white robe hung from her shoulders to the floor. She raised her arms and slid her hood back away from her head. White hair, straight and thick, unraveled from a loose braid and fell past her waist. Her hands, clad in white gloves, were long and lean. The skin of her face was pale, like an icy pond on Bright Night. All these things were captivating, but for Tymon, what captured his attention the most were her eyes. They were the brightest pale blue, and cold as ice. There was no warmth there. She saw Tymon still standing, and her head arched backward.

Docha spoke, not realizing that, behind him, Tymon still stood. "Kindest Princess, we kneel before you in honor. We bring gifts. Most interesting gifts."

"I accept your honor, Docha. You recall the glory of my father's kingdom and grant me my rightful state. I allow you to remain in my presence." Her voice, thin and piercing, not high-pitched, not loud, filled the room and their ears. "Continue," she said to Docha, without taking her gaze from Tymon.

Docha lifted bright blue bags from his pack and spread them at her feet on the dais. Quickly, he tugged at strings and pulled the bags open, spilling glittering gems onto the polished surface before her. Bright, clear sunlight caught them and spread beams of color randomly about the room. She did not look at the gems at all.

Micha took a chance and glanced upwards. He saw her drift from the dais, descending to the marble floor where they all knelt. He saw that Tymon still stood. The princess was moving Tymon's way. From the corner of his eye, Micha watched her flow around the perimeter of the group and approach Tymon. The boy was awestruck and swiveled his head to stare at her.

Docha now realized what was happening and attempted to put things right. "Kindest Princess! We bring these gifts for you as well." He swept his arm, indicating vaguely the area the companions were kneeling. "They, uh, not know of you, not know of you beauty, you wisdom. They not know…"

"They do not know of ME?" Her voice rose in disbelief.

"Of course, they know *now*. We, uh, I make them know, tell of You and your wonderfuls and kindnesses and…"

"What are they?" She wrinkled her nose. "This one looks damaged." As the princess came closer to Tymon, the boy was forced to lean back to continue to see her face. From the dais she did not look as tall. She did not bend to see Tymon closer. Micha watched and witnessed perfection in her regal bearing and robes but sensed only shabbiness in Tymon and the other companions.

"We are from the village, Princess, the one below the mountain, the one the King built for us long ago. Perhaps it is *your* village now?" Tymon's voice did not quaver in fear. Rather, he spoke with reverence and respect.

Docha quickly said, "Kindest Princess! They not know that to speak is forbidden. I tell, but they still not know! I say…"

"Silence, Docha. I will let this one speak." The princess' voice was icy cold, smooth, and firm. "Tell me, little one, what do you seek? Are not my father's gifts to your people enough? Why do you dare to enter his castle and my presence? Have you come to serve me?" Her voice intensified with each question.

Tymon, seeming to realize he overstepped a boundary, now looked about. He saw the others kneeling, and Micha caught his eye. A subtle wave of his hand indicated that Tymon should kneel also, but the princess' voice pulled the boy's gaze back upwards.

"DO NOT LOOK AWAY FROM MINE EYES! I give you no permission!" Her arms swept out and away from her body. Long flowing sleeves of crisp, glittering cloth hung straight and long like wings. "I grant you the power to answer my questions and no more. You are mine until I release you!"

Persa whimpered, cowering beneath the hood of her cloak. Docha fell to his knees once again. The other dwarves were still and silent as stones, heads pressed against the smooth, cold floor.

"I apologize, my Princess," Tymon said. "I do not mean to be disrespectful. I am just a boy, and I have never met someone like you."

"Someone *like* me? Do you think there are others like ME?" An icy edge tinged her words.

"I do not know, my Princess. I never knew there was such beauty in the world until I saw you."

For a second time, the princess' head arched back in surprise at Tymon. "You...a one-eyed little mouse, call me beautiful?" Her tone became reflective, and she lowered her arms.

"Perhaps there is a greater word for you, but it is the only one I have, my Princess."

The giant princess stood in silence for a moment. Micha counted forty breaths, but they were rapid. She spun silently, her gown and cloak floating out and away from her form, flowing in silent billows behind her as she again mounted the dais. A throne was in the center, and she took her place upon it. "Do you have a name?" She indicated Tymon with one long, slender finger.

"Yes, my Princess. I am Tymon."

"Tymon One-Eye...I see. And yet you have a vision of my beauty that none other dares to speak." Here, she glanced coldly at Docha.

"Kindest Princess," Docha began. "My Princess, I only bring you..."

"You bring me beautiful things, Docha. Do you feel I need enhancement? Am I not beauty enough? Is not my presence sufficient for you and your tribe? Do you not gain repast at my existence? When you find beautiful gems, is not your first thought how pale they are in comparison to me? My father's glorious castle frames me and gilds the sight of its Princess. Yet you bring me things! I am THE Princess! Though all have weakly fled my father's absence, I alone remain to mark his rightful rule. I hold his place, and you are my subjects." Her imperious tone softened. "My only subjects, and I know that you remain out of loyalty to him, the King who left us. Now you bring me a new kind of gift. You bring me more subjects. By the look of them, they are hardly worthy of me. Damaged, wounded, dirtier than you and your band. I may *yet* become cross at this pale offering. But. You have brought me Tymon One-Eye, and I believe I may find a way to be pleased." The royal tone of command returned. "Approach my father's throne, Tymon One-Eye."

The boy moved to her, entranced. Slowly he mounted the tall steps, his legs stretching to gain each new level. At the top step, just before the level of the throne, the princess reached to Tymon, laying her long fingers against the side of his face. He halted, gazing at her face, not turning away from her touch.

Micha kept his eyes on the scene, sensing that both Para and Camber were shifting slightly. He did not want them rushing to Tymon's aid against the actions of the giant princess. He did not know how the dwarves might react to such a course. A conflict did not seem advisable.

************

The princess stroked the boy's hair, and with a press of her thumb pushed away the filthy bandage. Tymon may have flinched, or it may have been that the princess' touch forced his head to one side. She pursed her lips, glancing at Docha.

"Not merely damaged, but diseased as well. What, Lord Docha, were you thinking in this action? Did you believe I might restore sight to this mouse as I once did for you?" Docha did not speak but rose, standing straight in the presence of the princess.

"I will not," said the princess. "Your wound, Lord Docha, was sustained in my defense. Little Tymon One-Eye, by your own words, did not even know of my existence until this present day. I will heal the wound to the extent that it will not deal him death or further sickness, for he is sick from this wound, though someone has provided him with adequate healing until now. Their technique will fail but has allowed him thus far to gain my presence. And in my presence, he sees my beauty. With only one eye. This is why he shall receive my mercies."

The princess asked many questions and made many statements but did not wait for answers or comments. Micha wondered if she knew there were others in the room, or if she spoke to herself often.

Micha had been watching Tymon, but he now saw Camber slowly unsheathe his knife beneath his cloak. Some trust had been gained, but Camber still was a question in Micha's mind. There was more history of mistrust than faith in their relationship. He noted Camber was watching the edge of the room where shadows formed behind the pillars. The light of day was paler now outside the room. Inside, there was a slight change, but the polished marble of the floor reflected the light, dispelling any shadows those in the center of the room might have cast.

Micha looked to Para and saw she too was watching the shadows behind the pillars. Her knife was already loose and in her hand. If Para and Camber both were preparing for danger, Micha too must get ready to stand with them. What did they see? What peril did they sense? Micha cast his eyes about, wondering how they would fare in a battle here. There was no place to hide, and he did not know where to run in retreat.

"Tymon One-Eye, did my dwarf lord tell you of his own injury, the one that near cost him his own sight?" Before the boy could respond, she continued. "He battled for my honor, and in the fight took a blow meant for my heart. An arrow shot from afar, deadly to mine self only." She looked at Docha and released a thin smile. "Lord of the Mines he was then, and it was not his battle. He leapt, a height higher than you may believe a dwarf can attain. He received the assassin's arrow across cheek and brow, the fierce iron tip scarring that dark skin and taking his sight in a cruel fashion. I took the battle that day, I and my warriors who followed my command. I..." she paused, looking at Docha, then continued, "We did not allow the archer to retreat successfully.

"I consulted my father's knowledge and with mine own skill returned Lord Docha's sight to him. Only I left the scar as a badge, an example of what a loyal subject of my father's kingdom should do for the line of succession. You call me your Princess, Tymon One-Eye? Do you mean this, or do you speak from fear?"

"I am not afraid, my Princess." Tymon's voice was small and difficult for the others to hear after the intensity of the Princess. "Well, I am afraid, a little. You are powerful, and I am small. I am afraid I have little value to you."

Micha heard Tymon's words but was no longer paying full attention to him. Sensing movement in the deepening shadows, he allowed his hunter's eyes to observe the chamber. The dwarves, on their knees still, and bent over at the waist with their heads down, were unmoving, and seemed to be unaware that others had somehow entered the room. Micha lay three fingers on the ground, then two. Para and Camber both lay two fingers down. Micha knew he had their attention and began to look about.

What could the intruders be after? The gems on the dais? The princess herself? There appeared to be nothing else of value in the vast room at all. So they must prepare to defend the dais itself. There was no cover. Micha subtly pulled the ties of his cloak loose from his neck and watched as Para and Camber followed his example. Their cloaks now rested on their shoulders but would come loose when they moved. Slowly, imperceptibly, he unslung his pack and worked it to his front. Gripping the straps in his hand, the pack rested on his forearm, ready to act as a shield. The light in the room faded as ambient sunlight turned to dusk.

"I cannot restore your eye, Tymon. I confess, too much time is past. Yet your good eye is better than many I know. I do not know what to do with you. Docha says you are all a gift. A gift of what I do not know. Your value escapes me at the moment."

************

While the princess spoke to Tymon, twelve figures detached themselves from the shadows, moving quietly toward the dais, their stealth creating suspicion and alarm in the minds of Camber, Para, and Micha. Why were they here? What did the intruders want? Why move in silence, unannounced, and, so far, unnoticed by the others? Micha wondered if he should sound alarm. Where did his loyalty lie? How far did it extend to the princess?

Micha did not completely understand the setting sun nor the swift nightfall upon the mountain top. He only knew that something was skulking from the shadows towards his friend, Tymon, and he did not know the motive. Docha was Micha's friend, and Docha's loyalty to the princess was enough for the young man to act in loyalty to her as well. But Docha apparently was not seeing what Micha and the others saw.

A glint of blade, the tip of a spear carried upright by the shadowy interlopers caught Micha's eye. Micha moved, and Para and Camber followed. They leapt to the dais, forming a minimal defensive ring around Tymon and the princess. The shadowy figures revealed themselves to be armed giants. In the waning light, twelve giants rushed the throne toward the princess.

In a swift breath, Micha saw Docha's face, surprised and frightened. The dwarves, uncertain of what was happening, rose, drawing their own weapons, and hesitantly began to step toward the dais. In that moment, Micha believed that they were allies in defense of something he could not even imagine mere days ago. In retrospect, Micha realized that the dwarves' weapons were turned toward him and his friends.

The giants swept past the dwarves, lowering their spears, tips aiming at the three defenders. Para leapt up toward the lead attacker's face. Lithe and light, she soared past the point of his spear, her feet landing on the shaft, forcing it downward. Using momentum, she increased the speed of her attack, thrusting her knife at his throat. He fell backward, but Micha could not see if he was wounded.

To his left, Micha heard a low growl. A knot of five giants were trying to attain the dais, and Camber was engaging them in battle. Camber disappeared from sight in the midst of the giants. Micha heard their lances clashing together as they sought to use them in close quarters. It was a futile effort. Micha heard their cries of pain and saw their clumsy retreat. The giants had tried to impale Camber and succeeded only in tripping themselves up.

Two giants approached Micha more cautiously. They dropped their spears and drew swords. Micha's knife was strong and sharp but no match for a sword blade. Shifting the pack on his arm to the fore, he launched his own attack. Leaping from the dais, sliding forward, dropping to his knees and slashing at their legs caused his opponents to become tangled in their own long weapons, as they sought to slay the little thing that threatened their ankles. By instinct, the giants jumped aside.

Micha's knife, sharp as it was, also proved no match for the thick leather boots and leggings they wore, but he disorganized their charge. Those giants became obstacles to the two giants who followed. Springing upward, Micha came down heavily on their feet. He was satisfied that bones were being broken. As the giants toppled over, crying out in pain, he moved to Para's assistance.

The first attacker she engaged was scrabbling backward, lacking his spear, which spun about on the smooth, polished stone floor. It tripped one poor fellow, and as he lost his balance, Para wrested his spear away and began rushing and jabbing at the others, one at a time. The sight was incongruous, a slight little human holding four armed giants at bay. Micha could see her struggling with a spear longer than she was tall, but the ferocity in her eyes was a beautiful sight to him.

A sound filled the room. Not a scream, though it was high in pitch. Not a cry, though there was a gasp of breath, like a sob. The princess' voice cut through the din. She said loudly, "OH...ENOUGH!"

Micha turned, as did they all, and saw her holding her sides and laughing. "Stop!" she cried. "Before one of you hurts themselves! Oh Lord Docha, my friend, what a great gift you bring me!"

On the far side of the dais a yelp of pain was followed by a low growl, and one of the giants that attacked from Camber's side scurried back, crablike, and away from the throne, joining his fellows as they huddled together just inside the shadows of two pillars. The princess laughed anew.

Cautiously, Micha moved away from Para and toward Camber. He called to his friend, "Camber. Brother. Come to us. Let us regroup."

For his part, Camber looked in greater control than when the Others attacked the dwarf camp. His eyes were wild and his chest heaving, but the bestiality of his attack was leavened and directed. Still, there was a fair amount of blood spilled on the floor. Micha thought it must all belong to the attacking giants, for Camber seemed clean of any gore.

************

The companions came together, looking upward at the throne. Tymon stood, blade out, in front of the giant princess. She noticed him and smiled. "None shall pass my defender, Tymon One-Eye!" There was mirth in her voice, but also warmth. "My defenders! How you have failed, and yet I feel richly rewarded."

"We did not fail!" Para said sharply. "We have them at bay, Princess!"

This elicited a chuckle, and the princess raised the back of her hand to her face. "Indeed, young one, and if I were referring to you, I would be in need of your correction. I must point out to you that you have defeated these twelve, my so-called defenders. Three human children. And had any of the twelve survived and made it past you three mighty little creatures, they surely would have perished at Tymon One-Eye's hands." Tymon alone remained with his weapon drawn and in defensive stance between the princess and all the others in the great throne room. She laid her large hand gently on the boy's head.

"Would that mine father could know of his humans' bravery! I have judged your kind harshly in the past. Now, you show me loyalty, and yet I see no reason. Why do you act so? Your value is perhaps deeper than I once believed. Are all humans such as these, Lord Docha?"

Docha approached the princess. "Not all humans, Princess. Not most. Yet some. These ones, few others, but we pledged…" He seemed embarrassed. "We pledged to King to care for such. We care for You also. Is our pledge to We. They like We in ways. They like You in ways. This one," Docha nodded at Micha, "he strong in that way. He see the mountain. He see the light. He see first, then they. He point. They see. He lead. He come look for King. I not know why." Docha shrugged. "We find They and bring to You. Here they be. All blood-of-dragon humans."

The laughter was gone from the princess. "All? Even this one?" She pointed to Camber. "I have seen his kind before. A great battle was fought because of this kind. Do you recall, Lord Docha?"

Docha rubbed at the scar on his face. He looked at Camber. "Blood of wrong dragon, kind Princess? Docha make mistake? I should make good?" He held his staff in an odd position. Micha thought he held it like a weapon. The light from the floor and walls was not bright, but Micha thought the tip of Docha's staff might be glowing.

The princess, stepping forward with her hand still upon Tymon's head, said, "The same as them but different? Lord Docha, you do not make such mistakes, but this one, he is a puzzle." She walked to Camber and leaned closer to his face. Gazing into his eyes she said, "No mistaking the light in his eyes. Red and angry. But there is more, is there not, Docha?"

Camber stepped back, looking away, but the princess' arm snaked forward, catching his face in one long, strong hand. "Did I say look away? I did not!" She dragged the boy's head back to face her.

Micha started forward, but Tymon, right at her side, said, "Kind Princess..."

Camber was pulling away by leaning backwards, but the princess held fast. She looked to Tymon, and Micha saw the fierce flashing of her eyes. Tymon kept his eye upon her for a good few moments. Then, turning to Camber, said, "Please, Camber, allow the Princess to see you. If she can help me and my wound, perhaps she will find kindness to grant you some healing."

Camber relaxed at Tymon's words, but the princess did not. "I am not to be a barter and trade vessel, one-eyed mouse." Her words were angry, but her tone was less so.

Tymon stood his ground. "My apologies, kind Princess. I am confused often and am not yet used to being in your royal presence."

Micha also relaxed, but the stress of preparing to defend Tymon, and then having the threat removed again and again was wearing on his already overloaded mind.

The princess whirled away from Camber. Micha saw red marks on the boy's face from where the long fingers gripped him. Camber did not look as if he were angry, as if he might shift, but he also did not look happy.

The giant princess walked into the center of the room, her gaze flashing about. Some of the giants were still upon the floor, three suffering from Micha stomping their feet and two stunned from Para knocking them down. Para still maintained a grip on the purloined lance, holding it at the ready.

"GET UP!" The princess yelled, and echoes bounced about the great, domed chamber. Outside, the sound of cracking ice and falling snow came to their ears.

Balled fists, hunched shoulders, eyes squeezing tight to narrow slits, the princess screeched, "Lord Docha! What are you thinking with this 'gift' that you bring? The gift of chaos and filth! What did you imagine? That I would somehow be grateful for their impudent presence? Have I wronged you in some fashion that you seek to plague me with living things that mean so little they will naught be missed by their families and fellow hovel dwellers? What possible rationale could bring you the belief that these beings who exist with vermin and mud could ever decorate my life with any favor?"

Docha stood as tall as he could while she ranted. When she paused for breath he said, "You light beacon. They see. They search for You. Beacon is for people find

You, Princess. You light. They see. You call. They come. They and We."

The princess stopped her rant and stared hard at the dwarf, her chest heaving with unspent rage, her skin ruddy, stark against her white hair. Pointing at Docha she said, "You! You dare speak…You are not my…I AM THE…Princess. I am the daughter of the King. You…" Her voice weakened. "You serve me, Lord Docha. You…" She staggered a little.

Tymon sprinted to her side. "Kind Princess, may I help you to your throne?" And without a word, she allowed the boy to lead her up the steps of the dais and sat heavily on the stone throne.

Docha approached her, but he did not kneel nor bow. "I serve you because I serve the King. Say so and We remove They from your sight. They go. We go. You, Princess, all alone again." He turned and beckoned to his fellows. Without hesitation they gathered to him. He turned to Micha. He whistled soft, three notes, then two. Micha turned to the dais and looked for Tymon. The boy was looking at him. Two notes sounded, an echo of the final two offered by Docha. Para whistled the notes and joined the dwarves, looking at Micha and Camber expectantly. Then she saw her sister.

Persa still lay on the floor. Before Para could walk to her, the princess said, "Stay. Please. Please stay." In the stiff silence that followed Docha's comments, the princess' voice was low but carried well. "Please. All of you. Remain as the guests of the castle of the King." She turned to look at Tymon, and said, "Please, be my guests."

Docha hesitated a moment before approaching the throne again. When he did, he walked straight and tall once more. But when he arrived at the edge of the dais, he bent at the waist in a courtly bow. "Highness. We," he waved his arms back to encompass everyone in the room, "feel honored by your request for our continued presence in your domain." The oddness of Docha using words in full sentences was almost one too many odd things for Micha to comprehend.

"You have my gratitude, Lord Docha, now and always. Forgive my doubting you. Or the virtues of your gift. Gifts, that is, though I fear in the disorder of the last few moments some of your fine gems have been ill-treated." She stood and walked to where a few of the glinting stones lay, having been kicked aside in the melee. "Gather these," she commanded to the knot of five giants still standing where Camber had forced them to retreat. Given something easily understandable to act upon they embraced their task and crawled about on all fours, snatching the gems from wherever they were flung.

Micha saw the princess look at the giants and heard her sigh softly, "Like beasts." She turned to him and also to Para. "And what of *these* gems? Unpolished, perhaps, but with virtue and fire deep inside. You are not a gift to keep, then? Something to treasure by enhancing your luster and releasing it back into the world to shine a pale fire in the darkness of your village's existence? Or shall you remain as my wards, my students, my charges? A responsibility for me to refine and guide? It is too weighty a decision to make this night or in haste. My mood is not conducive to favor or long sight. I fear a harsh decision may emerge that will be regrettable in the morn."

# 7

# THE MOON POOL

WHILE THE PRINCESS SPOKE, Docha lowered his head. The dwarf was saying something over and over. His voice was so low that Micha was not certain anyone could hear beyond the arm's length that separated him from the dwarf. The princess continued talking, and it may have been important, but Micha was striving to hear and make sense of Docha's mumblings. Suddenly, the princess stopped speaking. The room went silent. Almost. All that could be heard was Docha's voice.

"I can hear you, Lord Docha, but your meaning is unclear. Are you repeating, 'Moon Pool' over and over? Are you seeking to influence my decision with your unsubtle whispers?"

"Moon Pool for decisions, Princess. Make clear sight when King no clear in mind. Say future often. Help you now."

"It is past full moon, Docha. Three days only will the Moon Pool grant clarity of visions. It will not work tonight."

Docha consulted his staff. "Runes show Moon strong four nights. Weak first. Still full. Strong next and next.

Weak four, but still strong, still full. We on four. Moon Pool strong. Maybe? Strong enough for They? Maybe?"

The princess made annoyed sounds and pushed herself up from her throne. She paced a few steps left, then right. One of the five giants tasked with retrieving the scattered gems approached her without permission. Without ceremony, he handed her the gathered crystals all jumbled together. It was all she could do to maintain a hold on the gems and prevent them from tumbling again to the floor. She swiftly pulled upon her gown, creating a makeshift pouch for the stones, which came to rest near her abdomen.

She looked down at the gems, looked out across the throne room, now scattered with dwarves, human children, and fallen giants. She looked at her own gown and if there had been a mirror would have examined her own form in detail and felt disapproval at the image. Her regal throne room had become, in one short passage of time, a palace of disarray. Eyes wide, she shook her head and sought to end this messy evening. But regaining control was not yet to be for the princess.

"Docha wrong. Princess say 'No Moon Pool' so no Moon Pool. We sleep. We wait. Next moon. Full in twenty-eight…"

"No!" The giant princess spoke suddenly, resignation in her voice. "We will consult the Moon Pool over their fate, Docha." She attempted to clap her hands twice. The sound was muted by the cloth gathered to hold the crystals. "Captain of the Guards, prepare to proceed to the Tower." The giants gathered in a ragged line. The princess sighed. "Is it possible that one day you will learn the meaning of 'straight'?" She addressed them directly. They shuffled a bit, and one of them fell over clutching a swollen, possibly broken, foot. Her sigh was heavier then.

"Um, yer highness? Princess Frosti? Which tower do you mean?"

"Wha...*You dare*...in front of these...*my NAME!* What do you mean, 'Which tower?' The one with the Moon Pool at the...oh, Lord Docha, would you and your men kindly take the lead, please? The captain will follow at length..."

One of the other giants stepped forward, elbowing the captain out of the way and saying, "I know the way Fros...er, Fresc...Princess! I will lead! It is my turn to be captain anyway!" And without further discussion, he snapped his fingers at his fellows and called, "Fall In!" which they attempted to do and began an unsteady march toward the door.

The princess, dwarves, and the companions all watched them march out into the hallway and off down the long corridor, the giants never once looking back to see if they were being followed. Silence followed as the princess stared after her proclaimed defenders.

Tymon approached her and held open one of the blue bags that once held the gems Docha offered her. Without a word the princess poured them from the fold of her gown into the sack. Taking the sack from Tymon, she lay it on the arm of the throne. Gathering herself, smoothing the gown, adjusting her hair, she turned to Tymon. "No more fighting tonight. Tymon One-Eye, you are my sole protector this evening." She cast a frosty gaze at those remaining in her presence. "No one else approaches me unless I speak directly to them, is that understood?"

Everyone left in the room looked about uneasily, not sure if they should answer. The princess did not wait for a resolution to their dilemma. She strode away towards the great hallway. Tymon was at pains to keep up with her long stride, but the boy scrambled and kept just to her side and slightly behind.

************

The giants were well down the hall and nearly out of sight of those remaining as the princess exited the throne room. The dwarves followed swiftly. Micha and Para looked at one another. Camber came close. There in the center of the floor at Para's feet lay Persa, curled into a small ball. Soft sobs came from beneath her cloak. Para bent to her sister. She jumped at Para's touch. Micha and Camber flanked the sisters as Para lifted and cradled Persa.

"Persa, it's alright. I am here. Para is here with you. Tell me your fear, little sister." She spoke in a sing-song pattern, and Micha knew she had done this before. Poor Persa, he thought, so small and so many changes in a short time. He was barely able to keep it all together himself.

"No more fighting, Para! Please, make the noise and fighting stop! I am so scared." Persa's eyes were red and her face wet with tears. She looked at Para and clung to her sister's sleeve. "Don't leave me, Para! Don't leave me behind! Don't go with Da! He wants you to come. He wants his favorite girl, but I need you too, Para. Please don't go away."

Para pulled Persa close and sang little phrases, making comforting noises. She hummed and cooed like a mother to her baby. She stroked Persa's face and head until the girl regained her composure. "I am here, Persa. I am here. We are all here, and we will not leave you."

From the entry, Docha gave a small cough. Micha rose and walked to him. Docha spoke low. "Eh, we go. SHE not wait. SHE say come, but You stay? But We go? Girl go? Sooner better. Now good. Before best."

"Persa is frightened. She has been through a lot, Docha. We all have, but she is not as strong as We." A series of low whistles came from far down the hall. Docha responded, and the echo was pure. One tone came back.

"Eh." Docha cocked his head to one side and raised an eyebrow in surprise. "Kyniko come. He carry girl. A surprise, that. Kyniko no like anybody. Girl kick him in teeth, and he like girl. Who knew? I should kick him in teeth too maybe?" Docha laughed at that, and they went back to Persa.

Micha stroked her hair to get her attention. "I'm sorry, Micha," Persa said. "I am so weak. You should have left me in the village."

"Not so weak, little sister," Micha said. "You traveled far. You helped heal Tymon. You went to battle with trolls. And it seems you have a new friend in Kyniko. He is coming to carry you."

"Carry me like I am a burden, Micha."

"No. You are one of us. We are together. Together we found the mountain. Together we met the princess. Together we go into the future. Alright? I need you to be strong, but sometimes you can be afraid too. We just fought giants. Did you see?" Persa nodded yes. "Believe me, we were all scared!"

"I wasn't scared," Para said.

Kyniko arrived. Persa smiled at him. He knelt down and indicated she should climb on his back again. Persa stood.

"Thank you, Kyniko. I can walk if you'll walk next to me." The girl took the dwarf's hand, and he stood up. Docha laughed and Kyniko made some grumpy noises. But he did take Persa's tiny little hand in his large hairy hand, and together they walked the way the princess had gone.

Micha counted breaths again. The night sky should have made the giant's castle deeply black inside. Instead, the floor and ceiling glowed with a soft, pale light. Outside the sky was luminous with sparkling stars. Micha and Camber walked in wonder. Preest told them about Sun and Moon often. He rarely mentioned stars.

"Stars, Micha! I saw one!" Camber spoke low as they traversed the long hall. "The other night by the river, the clouds parted, and I saw a star. I didn't remember what they were. Look outside! Look at all the stars! What does it mean, Micha? The clouds are showing us the sky again. What does it mean?"

"I do not know. I find that I do not know a lot of things anymore, Camber." They walked on, trailing the rest. Soon they came to a grand staircase. The giant guards were no longer in sight.

Tymon gamely kept pace with the princess' long strides. The stair steps, proportioned for giants, proved daunting to the boy. Using the ornate railing with its carved posts, he was able to pull himself upward without delaying the princess' progress.

At the sight of the staircase, Persa moaned. Sensing Persa's weariness, Kyniko simply scooped her into his strong arms. She acquiesced. The pair, dwarf and human, started up the stairs. Close behind, five silent dwarves scrambled upward. The sight might have been funny, seeing the shorter beings struggling with the giant's steps, but no one was laughing. Too many days without adequate sleep left Micha, Para, and Camber too weary of heart and brain to see humor in their very foreign present reality.

Camber went next, followed by Docha and Para climbing side by side. Micha brought up the rear. He looked back down the long corridor. The far end, where they originated their walk, lay in shadow. Only the nearby space at the base of the stairs remained lit. Micha wanted to wonder at the source of light, but the effort was too great. Closing his eyes for a moment, he sought to recall the forest floor. The stone beneath his leather boots was hard and cold. The forest far away. Opening his eyes again, the boy took a deep breath and followed after the others. Behind him, all was stony silence.

************

The grand staircase led to a wide balcony. From there, a smaller, circular staircase spiraled upwards and through the ceiling. They climbed single file. Micha ran his hands along the metal railing, marveling at the ornate patterns, wondering about the skill and time that went into such a thing, pondering the great skill and long ages of time that must have passed in the creation of the cloud castle.

They were in a tower. Massive stone blocks made up the walls, and the stairs wound around, leaving the central cylinder open from bottom to top. The metal rail that kept someone from falling was made for beings larger than dwarves and humans. Micha clung tightly to it, but this meant reaching upwards with his arm. Part of the way up, his shoulder began to ache. He paused and looked upwards to the others. None of the dwarves seemed to need to hold the rail, and Para was slender enough to be able to walk close to the wall, granting herself safe distance from the edge. Camber also walked without need of the railing, adopting a four-footed approach to the stairs, leaning forward, and using his hands and arms to balance and propel his body.

Tall, thin windows exposed the night sky. Crisp, cold air sliced through the narrowing keep. Micha did not mind looking to the top. He could see his friends. One by one, they were exiting the tower. He tried to avoid looking down. Dim light shone at the base, and he could hardly believe they climbed such a distance. The symmetric swirl of the steps was hypnotic, and he found that if he did look down, the only way to allow the accompanying dizziness to pass was to press his back against the stone wall. His breath became shallow.

His ascent concluded at a flat foyer. The tower interior continued up to a peak. The foyer opened to the outside, and wind cut through a tall, slender portal. A thick, wooden door hinged with iron lay open. Micha saw his friends crossing a stone bridge. The mountain wind pushed hard against him, and his cloak whipped and snapped. He saw Para had tied her cloak tight around her middle, but the hood would not remain around her head in the fierce wind.

Stepping onto the long, stone bridge, Micha felt a wave of dizziness. The passage was wide, but there were no walls or barriers to contain him. To his left and right, the mountain fell away. The stone walls of the castle were discernible beneath the dome of the night sky, bright with stars and clear to the horizons. Thick clouds floated below, roiling and shifting. The light of Moon offered a view of a world vaster than any Micha imagined. Even Preest's wildest tales of open skies and massive seas did not prepare Micha for the reality he now beheld. Everything spun and swirled in the expanse. Micha felt minute and insignificant.

He stood gripping the side of the doorway, feeling like he may just fall away from the bridge if he stepped forward. The wind tugged at him. He felt the rush of frigid air, imagining how it would feel if he simply stepped over the edge. One slip and he could return to the earth and forest far below. Would he fall through the clouds? Would they stop him from plummeting hard into the earth and trees?

He stared into the abyss. His pulse sounded loud in his ears. He could hear his heart and breath quickening. An image of wings, leather and bone, rose unbidden in his mind. A leap, and a moment for the wind to catch and carry the flier upon the currents of air. Could his cloak act as wings? Was he leaning too far? The world spun. His knees grew weak, his calves heavy. The night was brightening, and Micha did not know if his eyes were open or closed.

A sharp, strong yank at his cloak brought awareness. Para stood next to him, deep concern in her eyes. "You are with us. We go together. Not that way. Take my hand." She held her hand out but did not reach for his. Only when he reached for her did she clasp his hand tight. Together they walked along the stone bridge, slow at first, then faster to catch the others.

At the end of the bridge a large circular arena positioned atop another larger tower. The circular crown of the flattened tower was large enough that the princess' current court was able to gather without crowding one another. Several braziers were lit and possessed iron covers so that heat flowed about, but not the firelight, leaving only circles of light with shallow shadows around the flat, stone roof. A vast array of stars offered subtle illumination that served to allow sight into the night. The stone floor was free of snow and ice from the brazier's warmth, still, the edges of the tower offered no protection for the unwary. A wrong step and a person would be lost to the world.

Persa and Kyniko stood near one the braziers. The dwarf cradled the girl in his muscular arms. Her face was buried in his shoulder. The other dwarves huddled around one another. Camber stood near them, but apart. The giants were spaced randomly in an approximate, but distinctly uneven circle near the unguarded edge. They did not appear affected by the cold and so did not seek access to the heating fires.

Moon's light gleamed off the icy mountain peaks that did show their points above the cloud banks below. There was no trace of ice or snow upon the flat plane of the tower. Micha wondered; what fire could keep such cold at bay? He felt gusts of warmth as he and Para approached the princess.

The princess stood in the center of the tower crown near to a vast metal grail. Inside the grail, a fluid rippled in the wind. Micha felt it could not be water, for it was not frozen. There was warmth about, but the wintry winds still blew fierce. What the fluid was, he could not guess. This, then, must be the Moon Pool, but he did not know what that meant.

He and Para pulled together, sharing the heat of their bodies as well as seeking some familiarity in the face of the strangeness they were experiencing. "I am so weary," Para said. "I wish we were alone again in the wood." Micha pulled her tight. They stood chest to chest, but both turned their heads to watch the spectacle of the giant princess and the Moon Pool.

\*\*\*\*\*\*\*\*\*\*\*\*

The princess' arms were raised. Uttering odd words, singing strange notes, crafting symbols with fingers, and making signs with her hands, she gazed upward to Moon itself. Micha tried to make sense of the ceremony. Preest would do similar things on various occasions. Mostly the rituals made sense or had some purported purpose. Harvest or planting, the beginning of a hunt or the expression of gratitude at the success of one, the birth of a child or the death of a villager. Micha never put much stock in the actions, never understood the reasons. Hunting and crops seemed to have success or failure in equal measure during his life, regardless of Preest's activities.

The fluid in the basin rippled, but that could easily be assigned to the winds. Everyone's cloaks or scarves snapped and whipped in the icy gusts. Moon was gaining height in the night sky. Preest's lessons came back slowly to Micha's memory. Moon went through phases and sometimes it was present and others it was not, sometimes large and round, sometimes small and shaped like a harvesting sickle. Around Gaia, Moon would travel, like a dance. It was a story Preest told, and there was never any reality to grant understanding, until now.

Micha watched a great white orb rising, wide and fat at the horizon, growing smaller as it gained height in the rich, night sky. Patterns upon the orb, darker and lighter patches, made no sense, but little did in the giant's castle.

Lord Docha approached the princess, moving slow and soft. She was speaking a language Micha never had heard. Turning at Docha's approach, she said, "Perhaps the power of the pool is spent, Lord Docha. There is no response."

"Power of Princess strong," Docha said. "Power of Moon? Moon there." He pointed upward. "Princess here. We wait."

"For what, Docha?" She spoke quietly but Micha heard her clear. "A vision for these humans? Will the Moon Pool grant these short-lived ones such a boon?"

"For They, yes. For You, more. Seeking clarity. Seeking decision. Fate of humans in Princess' domain is question you ask. Not They."

She looked at the dwarf and nodded. Tymon stood near, gazing upward at the princess. "I should have taken time to clean you up, little mouse," she said to him, smiling. Looking around, she added, "All of you. I seek a vision of the future for these little forest creatures, Lord Docha. I will make the attempt once more. If I am successful, they must gaze into the pool and tell me what they see. I will know what to do by their visions. Stay close, Tymon."

She began the incantations once more. This time, there was a familiarity to their cadence, once heard, the sounds no longer so strange to Micha's ears. Docha stood close to the princess, occasionally shifting his staff in purposeful patterns, weaving the tip in a spiral, or using his fingers to make a sign upon the shaft.

The wind went quiet. The heat of the braziers flowed about evenly. No one added fuel to the fires, and once again, Micha pondered the source of such flame. The sound of the princess' voice softened until it was almost imperceptible. The fluid still undulated, but now there were definitive patterns occurring again and again. Circular ripples, pointed squares morphing into triangular wavelets, bouncing peaks tossing droplets high and receiving them as they returned to the pool. A high-pitched hum began to emanate from the pool. At least, that is where Micha believed it started. The sound soon filled the night. Micha could not identify a clear source.

Docha stepped back and glanced over to Micha. He raised his eyebrows and smiled a great grin. Bobbing his head towards the Moon Pool, he held a finger to his lips for silence. It was unnecessary. What was there to say? What questions could they possibly ask? None of the companions had ever heard of the Moon Pool until a short time ago.

************

All went still.

Time passing. Warmth emanating. Moon rising. At its zenith, the pool began to glow silvery white. Smiling, the princess lowered her arms. Her pale face glowed in the ambient light, her white hair gleaming. Her eyes were brilliant blue and silver. She began to bend over to look at the pool, but the smile fled her face before she completed the action. She did not frown, but rather leaned away.

Turning to Tymon, she said, "Look into the Moon Pool, Tymon One-Eye. Gaze and tell me what you see." Standing tiptoe, the boy looked over the edge of the grail.

"I see green. The forest and hills are bright green. All the trees! There are so many. They are full with leaves! They are no longer dying. The sky is bright. There is…is Sun yellow?" He looked at the princess and she nodded yes. "There is Sun, and I think we are all warm. I see Micha and Para. I see…" He raised his eyes again and looked across to Persa, held in Kyniko's arms.

"You see a future," the princess said. "Mind you, it is only a possible future, but your image is strong, especially for one whose sight is halved. Will you walk towards this vision, Tymon?"

The boy did not know how to answer. He said, "It is a pleasant vision, my Princess. I did not see you there." She laughed gently.

"I am there, Tymon. Seen or unseen, I am there. I have seen a future also, though I like it not. Will you walk towards the future you have seen, Lord Tymon?"

The boy drew himself up, standing as tall as he could. "It looks like a good future, Princess. I will walk that way if you wish."

"No, Tymon," she scolded him softly. "This must be your decision. Do not be afraid to decide where you wish to walk, even if it may be a mistake."

"I am not afraid, kind Princess. I will walk to this vision."

"We will walk together, Lord Tymon, even if we are apart."

The princess turned to Camber. "Come. You may gaze also, but only if you wish. You may like your vision even less than I like mine."

Camber stood still for a moment. He looked around and knew, despite words of acceptance and friendship, he was separate. He shivered, though not from cold. Approaching the Moon Pool, he asked, "What do I do?"

Tymon took his hand. "It is easy. You just look. Tell her what you see. I will stand with you if you want."

Camber took a breath. "Thank you, Tymon, but I believe I must stand…alone." He approached the Moon Pool, tilting his head to gaze into the silvery depths.

Camber's sight wavered. His eyes seemed to lose the light for just a moment. The same rush of energy was happening that had occurred in the battle of the dwarves' camp. He recognized this feeling, recalling when it first flowed.

He saw an image of his father lying dead on the floor of their rough home. His father's face was that of a beast, but slowly returning to the look of a human. His body shifted shape. Camber saw his own reflection just then and knew he too was in that bestial form. The image altered, and behind him he could see a dragon, massive and deep, bloody red. It reared its head and arched its long neck. Flame coursed from its body and turned into thousands of smaller bloody-red dragons. They all took flight and began attacking people. Sometimes, Camber thought he could see them actually becoming people. Again, he saw his own face.

Towns, large and clean with great populations, ran in terror. Camber watched himself walking down streets and alleys in the form of a beast. Above him, the sky flamed. He felt a thrill at the fear of others. He felt great rage. He longed to frighten and felt a roar grow within his chest.

He did not speak these images aloud.

Within the pool, patternless fluids trembled and shook, splashing and spattering, drops catching the ruddy orange light of the fires from the braziers.

The princess stood patient. She soon passed a long arm across the roiling fluids of the Moon Pool. "Enough of this," she said quietly. Camber's vision shifted again.

He too saw the green lands Tymon witnessed, but Camber saw them from a great height, as if he were in flight. Sun warmed him, and breezes cooled him. In his vision, he climbed higher until the green fields and forests were far below and the snowy mountain peaks surrounded him. The castle came into view. The tower top, the one they stood upon now, beckoned within his vision, though it was daylight. Banking about, Camber lowered gently to the surface. The princess was there, along with her Giant Court.

Camber was the only human around. He felt a deep grief pass through his core. Alone! He wanted to scream the word but had no strength. "Alone." The sound floated from his lips, more a moan than a word. He gave a deep sigh, expelling breath in a long steady rush. "Tymon," he said in a whisper, and little Tymon did his best to catch him as he slumped to the ground.

Micha and Para moved quickly to his side. Tymon was cradling Camber's head in his lap. Para grasped his hand. "Camber," she called softly. "We are here, Camber. Can you see us? You are not alone. We won't leave you." She spoke like she believed her words to be true.

But Camber knew a different truth. He let his eyes remain closed, saying, "I am happy you are all here now. Right now is enough."

"Tymon One-Eye, assist your friend to the side. There, by the eastern brazier. Remain with him until he is recovered." The princess' words were a command, yet her tone was gentle.

Camber stood carefully, his knees not co-operating. Tymon supported him as best he could, but he was too short to be of much real use. Two of the giant guards moved forward and took Camber's arms, holding and guiding him to the brazier the princess indicated. They helped him lie down, and Tymon knelt next to him. Camber lost consciousness. The flames in the brazier wavered and flared for a short time, though the winds were still. Camber stirred and twitched, but as the flames calmed, so did he.

"It is now your turn, Leader Micha." The princess intoned his name like a spell cast. She looked upward at Moon, as it dropped, nearing the horizon to the west. She said, "Quickly now, or the Pool will lose Selene's light." Micha did not understand exactly what that meant but felt the urgency. Approaching the Pool, he looked within.

Like Tymon he saw the golden yellow of Sun and lush greens of growth. He also saw the village, no longer decayed. Empty buildings now were full with life. In his vision, walls once fallen now stood strong and gleaming. People walked in the day and also in the night. A celebration, a faire, was in progress. Music played, stalls were busy and full with goods and crafts, crops were plentiful and Micha could smell the wafting scents of cooking in the air!

In the town center, the square that Preest said was the symbol of the Giant King, Micha saw himself standing atop a dais. He spoke to the town. He directed their work. He made decisions and gave advice. He laughed at the joys he saw. He swept newborn children into the air and smiled at their fresh, healthy faces. The sound of laughter mingled with song.

And all about he saw his own children, busy with play and tasks, stacking and carrying as their mother requested. Para was there with him, next to him on the dais, and they spoke and consulted with one another. The town was clean and clear of debris. Fresh water rose from fountains and wells. Men and women were trained in lost ways of healing and art. Across the lintel of a doorway leading to a large building were the words, "Wisdoms Shared." Inside, Preest stood in front of classrooms lined with shelves. Books and models were everywhere, and knowledge was given and discovered.

Witnessing these things, Micha knew them at a deep level to be truth, though he only understood the images in his heart and not his head. The images faded then, and he could hear the voice of the giant princess say, "You can gaze long at the dream, Micha, or you can return to us now and begin to live it."

Para took him by the hand. He smiled at her, but she only said, "It is my time, Micha. Now, before it is too late." He moved aside, and Para set her eyes on the surface of the pool.

Her vision came swiftly. She first saw the town as Micha had witnessed it, his vision echoed in hers, but then faded. It was replaced by an image of the town abandoned and in ruin. Weeds and vines sought to grow along the rubbled stone streets. Dead leaves blew about the dry fountains, choking the holes where water once flowed free. Dark skies refused the earth light. Clouds lowered, and weak rains drizzled cold on a dying land. No people roamed, and no sound of life was heard. She could see Giant's Mountain in the distance, and no light glowed from its peak. In her vision, she saw the princess, alone at the top of the mountain, refusing to look down, imperious and haughty. All around her, the castle also suffered decay and ruin. Even at this great height, clouds blotted out Sun, and the earth felt no warmth.

Para viewed the village again. Snow and ice were all about, winds tormenting any who ventured out of shabby shelters. The remnants of the villagers huddled in a small section of the old town. Walls were in disrepair. Wells were dry or weak. The people were without joy and carried little hope. Children died. In her vision, Micha, old and weak, sat alone on the edge of a broken-down wall. Small graves were in his sight, five of them, and the fifth one fresh. Stones stacked over bodies, for the earth was frozen and unyielding. Micha laid down next to the fresh grave. Para saw his life ebb, saw him fade, saw their world end.

"No," she wept. "NO! This cannot be. We must do something! YOU must do something! Princess! What can be done?"

"What you witness is a future. It is only a possible future, but your vision is strong. All things grow; all things fail. The light wanes, and Moon sets. See how the glow fades in the pool? Come. We will retire for the evening and discuss it afresh in the light of day." She stepped away from the Moon Pool and began to walk toward the stone bridge.

"Wait!" Tymon's voice stopped the princess.

She whirled angrily. "YOU DO NOT COMMAND! You may have my favor, Tymon One-Eye, but you do not rule!"

"My Princess," Tymon said, his tone contrite but his voice firm, "I did not mean to command you. Only, Persa did not have a chance. She should look too, shouldn't she?"

"The light is past now, Tymon One-Eye. She has lost her chance. Do not lose yours."

"My Princess." Tymon pressed on despite her glare. "If only you would stand just so and allow the light of Moon to be reflected by your great beauty, perhaps Persa could have just a small vision from the Moon Pool? Perhaps your own light would be enough to grant this favor?"

The princess shifted at the sound of the compliments. She thought a moment and looked to Moon. Stepping to the eastern side of the Moon Pool, she raised her arms slightly and let the voluminous sleeves catch the waning light. She leaned forward a bit, and the dark pool lit again with reflected light.

Rising from his station near Camber, Tymon wasted no time in running to where Kyniko held Persa. "Come, Persa. Quick! Do not waste this, or She will be cross!"

"No, Tymon! I'm afraid. Para was scared. Camber was scared. What if my vision is terrible? I can't." She whimpered and clutched at Kyniko.

"Come. I will look with you. We will see a vision together." Tymon tugged at Persa. Kyniko lowered her to the stone floor, urging her toward the Moon Pool. She approached, holding Tymon's hand. Together they leaned over the edge, each on tiptoe. Persa saw Tymon and he saw her. They stood together, side by side, holding hands. They stood like that for several moments until Moon set, full and wide across the western range of peaks. To the east, the sky brightened with the promise of the rising sun.

As they stepped away from the Moon Pool, they kept holding hands and smiling. Persa turned to face the princess. "What a beautiful vision. My thanks, kind Princess. I know now why Docha calls you such."

Gazing coldly at Persa, the princess said, "I saw nothing."

# 8
# CASTLE MAGIC

DOCHA LED THEM ALL BACK DOWNWARD, though Micha was not certain the stairs were the same as the ones they climbed last night. The hall at the base was shorter, and there were not as many windows as he recalled. No one spoke, though the dwarves did exchange some low-toned whistles. Camber walked, but needed assistance at corners and through doorways, as if he were asleep and unable to see such things as walls or comprehend that they should stay together. Several times, Micha sought to take Para by the hand. She jerked away and stepped faster. He had seen her like this before, but this seemed different, harsher.

"Take time," Docha whispered to him at one point. "Moon Pool not kind to girl. Kind to you mebbe? She know. She want kind like you. Moon Pool not truth. Moon Pool is Could Be Truth."

"What is it?" Micha asked. "How does it work? My vision was so clear. I could smell and taste what I was seeing."

"Best not dwell. Vision settle in sleep. Dreaming filter vision. SHE sleep. You sleep. No talking."

Micha did not think there would be much effort at conversation. His friends were dragging their feet. Kyniko carried Persa once again. The girl was deep in exhausted slumber. Udamon had swung Tymon upward as they entered the hallway, and the boy did not resist.

Docha stopped them at a tall wooden door and bade them enter.

A curtained room with piles of cushions all around and fires in braziers and hearths greeted the exhausted companions. Soft blankets and pillows kept them in comfort through the day and on into the next night. All slept, and all dreamt. Neither Camber nor Para woke, though their dreams were most disturbing.

The companions awoke late in the morning of their third day at the giant's castle. Micha roused earliest. The scent of cooking wafted from around a bend in a branch off the main hallway. He carefully noted marks on the floors and walls so as to be able to find his way back. The castle was massive in size, and labyrinthine. He was certain he would never find the way back to the sleeping chambers, let alone the cavern from whence they arrived.

A kitchen was alight with small fires in large hearths. Myshkin was there with his floppy hat and big grin. Boleslau and Udamon also. They greeted him with a wave and offer of a plate.

"No giants?" Micha asked, grinning.

"Giants scared!" Myshkin said. "You scary." He climbed on the table pretending to be tall, then looked at Micha and fainted away. Udamon and Boleslau laughed hard at his antics and Micha joined them.

The dwarves were cooking a variety of foods. The pantry and shelves were pulled apart. Micha had never seen so much food in one place. The dwarves piled a large metal plate full of eggs, breads, meats, and fruits. Micha started eating and did not stop until it was all vanished. Myshkin laughed and handed him more.

"We should save some for the others," Micha said. Udamon opened a door. Micha saw a pantry piled high with food.

"Whole castle magic," Udamon said. "King's magic. Food always in kitchen. Food always here. We always hungry. We always here! Here for SHE, yes. Here for We? Yes! Eat, eat!" And Micha did.

Camber came around the corner with Para. Despite the length of sleep time, she looked tired. Micha met her at the door, guiding her to a table. Her sleepy look vanished when he piled food in front of her. She ate without a word of greeting.

Without much sound Camber also dug into the plate Myshkin passed him. Docha arrived a little later with the others. Only Kyniko, Persa, and Tymon were absent.

"Kyniko awake. His friend still sleep. Her friend awake too. They stay with girl."

"I'll bring them some food," Camber said.

"No." Docha spoke nonchalantly, but firm. "Food magic here." He pointed to the floor. "No food magic there. They must come to food. Kyniko fine. One-Eye fine. He got smell! He be here soon. He drool."

Micha asked, "What happens now, Docha? Should I call you 'Lord Docha'?" Udamon laughed out loud while

Myshkin puffed up his chest and strode about, pointing, scowling, and acting the Lord, with exaggerated, incomprehensible commands.

"Nah Ha! No 'Lord Docha' no more!" Docha barked, not quite laughing. "No 'Lord Docha'. No more." He was quieter and Myshkin ceased his antics.

Docha chewed on a large roll for a moment, then said, "Now. Today. SHE will be scary. Always scary. You scared?"

"I was. You made her sound terrifying, Docha. She is not so frightening. Not like you say."

"No? Good for you. Today maybe SHE be scary. Maybe kind. SHE talk. SHE ask. Moon Pool is power. SHE no look at Her vision no more. No Moon Pool for SHE. SHE scared what she see. You say what you see. We see what SHE say. HA Ha ha." Micha wondered at Docha as he spoke in his odd pattern. That morning, for the first time, Micha thought it might be like a song, only spoken.

"Give true answer. SHE ask. You say Truth. You no hide. SHE see if you hide."

Kyniko came in with Persa and Tymon. Para, Camber, and Micha all stared at Tymon. His face clean and hair brushed, he now wore a dark leather patch over his eye, the filthy, makeshift bandage vanished sometime during their sleep.

Camber was the first to say, "Look at us!" And they did. All the companions now wore clean clothing, warm cloth of a fine weave. Strong buttons fastened shirts and cuffs. Leggings beneath trousers clad their calves down to their toes, and they each wore shoes of thick, soft leather.

"Look at us!" Tymon said, echoing Camber. Micha joined in, marveling as they noticed their hair washed and combed free of woodland debris, hands and nails clean, and all the small cuts and scrapes sustained in the various encounters of their journey now cleansed and treated.

"Wondered when you see you!" Docha said. "Look now like belong in castle!"

"Did you do this?" Tymon asked, pointing to his eye patch.

"ME? We? No. Is SHE. Magic in SHE. Good magic. You sleep. You safe. You heal. Clean. Rest. Now eat! Castle Magic. Princess' castle."

"How did we not notice this happening?" Para said sullenly. "How does she do such a thing without our permission?"

"Would you rather be filthy?" Micha asked, his voice pitched low for her alone to hear. "Would you have refused such an offer? Are you so proud as to not accept the hospitality of giants? It is what we always were told, Para. It is why we started on this path. It is what we want for all the village. Being ungrateful now may turn the princess against such a course." He was not unkind, but there was a curtness to his words. Para looked down at her plate and continued eating in silence.

Kyniko, Tymon, and Persa were served, and the conversation wandered to what food was best. After everyone was satiated, Docha said, "Now is good. We take you to SHE."

************

The way was some distance, and together Micha and Camber sought to make a trail to follow back. The sameness of the walls was maddening, and soon they both surrendered the task. The dwarves followed, though Docha led the way. Persa and Tymon walked with Kyniko and Myshkin. Para hung back but kept pace, not speaking or looking at anyone. A huge golden door opened as they approached. Inside, two of the twelve giant guards were pulling long ropes on pulleys to move the door.

This chamber felt considerably smaller than many of the others they had seen, though it still appeared vast. Darkness engulfed the far walls, and the ceiling lay in shadows. The princess sat in a large chair facing the doorway. To the right a marble wall was visible. To the left darkness, and shadows took hold.

Her guards waved the children forward. Chairs and cushions were in front of the princess' throne. The companions took their seats. It was not unlike sitting in one of Preest's classes, but the surroundings were far from the rustic nature of the village. Lustrous walls and gleaming sconces made this room bright. Candles and fires from the rough stone fireplace were all the light they had in the village. Wooden benches now were replaced with large, cushioned chairs, golden in color.

Camber looked around, peering into the shadowed areas. There were no open windows here. Dark drapes hung long, curling upon the floor. Lanterns and torches flickered yellow light, making shimmering patterns on the walls. In the deepest portion of the room, pale reflections glinted like many small mirrors. One lone red light glowed bright in the farthest corner.

The princess spoke, "Go now, all of the rest. I wish to be left alone with my Lord Docha's gifts." The giants reluctantly moved from the room, though three of them moved faster when Camber turned around and looked at them. The dwarves stood still for a moment, until Docha realized the princess had dismissed *them* also. They shuffled out, but at the last moment she relented, saying, "Docha. Stay."

"Tymon One-Eye, you choose to sit with this girl?" She pointed at Persa.

"I will sit where you wish, my Princess, but Persa is scared, and I thought I would stay with her for a while."

"She is scared, and I am scary? Is that what Docha told you? The rascal. He serves me well. I can be...specific in my requests, sharp. Truthfully, I well know he serves my father, the absent King. I am a princess only because I once was, not because I have a kingdom to rule. Docha is my loyal companion, and I treat him poorly at times. Is that not right, Lord Docha?"

"You kind always, Princess. I serve you. I choose such service. We choose."

"You speak well, Lord Docha, even if your words are not always as true as they might be." She smiled at him, and he gave an overly elaborate bow. "My father would be proud of you, Docha. Prouder of you than of myself. He would be very proud of you five, especially Lord Tymon One-Eye." Everyone heard the term "Lord" once again, placed in front of Tymon, and wondered what she could mean by it.

She went on, "My father would not be proud of what has happened to this world. But then, he left it, so he cannot complain. It was *His* world, I once believed. Reality is difficult to accept. Especially when it differs from one's beliefs. I believed my father to be a constant in the world. He would say to me, 'Daughter, the only constant is change.' I thought he meant everything *other* than ourselves."

"Where is your father?" Micha asked.

"They tell me he is no longer on the earth." She cast a cold eye towards Docha.

"We have as truth, kind Princess. Truth from Nicholaus."

"Mmmm, my kind uncle who always speaks the truth, but oft omits the truth around his speaking. Does he still run with that vicious little troll, Dark Piet? We should have killed him twice, Docha. Is kind Nicholaus the one who taught you to speak, Docha?" She looked away, waving her hand about in dismissal.

"Ah! No matter to such as you five children. I digress like some old human crone. What to do with you, this is the matter we dwell upon. Docha brings you and says you are a gift. I suspect there are many layers to this dwarf logic, yet I am too idle to solve such a puzzle. Let us follow instead the visions obtained from the Moon Pool.

"You, Para, you were frightened by what you saw. You wanted *us* to do *something* about something. What would you have us do?"

Para stood. "It was a terrible scene, Princess. The world was wasted and all life too. Was it real? I don't want that future. Can we prevent it from happening? You must do something! You cannot let everyone die!"

Eyes growing cold, her voice intense, the princess said, "Already, your world is dying. I would not care to save it except for the fact that it means mine also will perish." Her tone was icy. "The world is what humans have made of it. Gaia has given the earth over to them and taken it from us, the giants, her first stewards after the dragons. If Gaia wants them to kill her off, what power do I have that is stronger than the All Mother?"

Para's voice matched the intensity of the princess as she asked, "Is there nothing you can do for us? You sneak into our sleep and clean and change us like infants, you heal our wounds, but have you no magic powerful enough to shift the world to a better place?" Para's tone grew fiery as she leaned toward the princess. "Are we *things* to you? No better than animals? Beneath your attention? Is that what your father taught you? Is the world of so little value to you that you will let it deteriorate while you sit alone in the clouds? Do you not have some magic to save the world? Are you so unwilling, so selfish, so uncaring that you are content to be isolated in this empty castle and pretend to be a ruler?"

Micha wanted to do something: make Para sit down, apologize, take back her challenging words.

Micha heard Docha say in a whisper, "Uh, oh. Scary start now."

The giant princess pulled her shoulders high, standing straighter, appearing to grow ever taller, seeming to rise from the floor. Her head tilted back, and she looked down her nose with icy eyes, freezing everyone in the room. Inhaling, it seemed to Micha that she left little air for anyone else to breathe. "Impudent forest beast! All I have done since you arrived unbidden in MY CASTLE is accommodate your needs! You should all be DEAD ALREADY! The forest should be eating your sparse corpses! I have given you a greater gift than any human before you, that of a vision of the future. YOUR FUTURES as you hope and as you FEAR! DO you not have hands? Have you no will? Do you not have FREE WILL? Is there no strength left in my father's pets? Can they no longer feed themselves? You wish for magic? You wish for rescue?  A return to some mythic golden age? Save your world? I AM A PRINCESS! Someone should be saving the world for ME!" She stood up, her arms waving about in anger. As she ranted, her white gown billowed and roiled like winter storm clouds. Her voice cracked like the summer thunders. Long white hair flared outward from her head like lightning bolts, her thick braid whipping about. The once beautiful room felt like a trap they may never escape. Everyone leaned back, bracing against the onslaught of her tone and words.

All save Tymon. Rising from his seat next to Persa, dressed now in finer clothes than he had ever seen before, well-fed by the mystical larder of a giant's castle, well-rested in bedding softer than what he could have dreamt of back in his aging, failing village, young Tymon placed himself between the princess and his friends.

"Princess." Tymon, small and brave, looked up at her. "How can I help you save your world?"

She paused in her rant to stare at the boy. The gown settled around her. The room quieted, and the walls ceased reverberating from the fierce tirade. The princess unclenched her fists, unhunched her shoulders, unsquinted her eyes, and took a long, slow breath. Standing straight once more, she smoothed her gown, adjusted her hair, and folded her hands together in front of her. She then looked at Docha.

After a lengthy pause, she said, "These *are* a gift, Lord Docha. They calm me. They humor me. They protect me, and now they wish to save *my* world. At least, Lord Tymon One-Eye does. Any others?"

Micha took a very deep breath, stood up, and bowed slightly. "Princess, we are only what you see. Our village, once your father's according to our traditions, is dying. We do not want that. We also do not want you to lose your world. We are threatened by strangers who seem to only want our deaths. We are cold always, and our food is scarce, getting more so by the day. We have plenty of wood, but only because all the trees are dying. The winter is long, and the summer never stays long enough for a season of growth to harvest. Water is grimy and unclean and does not rise easily to the wells.

"If it will help us, we will help you, and that is the way of things. But we will help also because it is in our nature to do so. The Others, they will not be so kind, not in our experience. We ask if you can do something. We ask because we do not know what to do. We hear that we once followed the guidance of a giant king. There are those who do not believe that giants even exist, not now or then. Yet, I believe that we, and not only us…" Micha indicated his friends, "…but all the village would again follow a giant if She chose to lead."

It appeared for a moment as if the rage would return. Her lips twisted, her cheeks twitched, her eyes fluttered, and her pale skin grew rosy red. Another deep long breath, however, allowed her to maintain her composure. Stepping back, but never turning to face away from the companions, the princess regained her seat.

"So, my Lord Docha brings me the gift of responsibility. You are a clever one, Lord Dwarf. It is a lesson that long has eluded me."

She sat gazing off at some distant sight, a time and place the others could not see. The castle faded from her sight, the children and Docha slipping away from her reality.

# 9

# PRINCESS PAST AND FUTURE

MISTS ROSE AROUND HER. She envisioned herself in the past, walking with her father once more. She heard her father's voice. Always, when she was alone, she could hear his voice, deep and strong, gentle with her, but powerful when others required guidance.

"I see an ending, and in the ending, I must see a beginning," he said.

Freschia looked at her father with saddened love in her eyes. "Do you not wish for a continuing rather than an ending?"

"Trees continue to drop their leaves in winter and sprout new buds in the spring. Even the largest tree falls to the continuance of time. When it falls, it continues, but no longer as a tree. I feel this beginning will not rise as high as even our ending."

His daughter turned her head, her long braid shifting across her shoulder. Her pale blue eyes glistening as she looked back upon their beautiful mountain. Already the mists descended over the tallest spires. The high paths were filling with swirling crystalline fogs.

Below was their valley, and from there the world had spread at their feet for many golden eons. Where once the highways were filled with trade and music, now the tracks were empty and overgrown. Here and there, Freschia could spot roving bands of the New Men. Even from such a distance, she could sense their fear.

How long her father had sought to raise them, instruct them, integrate them into society, and always they fought. They fought everything. They fought amongst themselves, they fought those near them, they banded together and traveled to find others to fight. They fought Gaia herself and would fight Sol if they could reach him. One day, she knew, they would try to fling their stones and spears into the realms above.

Her father was a mighty being, a son of the dragons and the first of the First Men. He had been roaming the globe since these New Men were living in trees. He carried the skills of dragonfire and freely shared light with any and all. He had given Gaia a great golden age.

Now Freschia's heart ached as she walked with him into the mists of history. She did not comprehend the "why" of it all. The New Men could be contained! Why must all this beauty lie fallow and wasted while these human beasts overrun the world?

\*\*\*\*\*\*\*\*\*\*\*\*

Time passed. The princess sat still, unmoving, eyes open, but seeing something other than the chamber she occupied. Unsure of what to do, Docha and the children sat in silence. Finally, Freschia, daughter of the Giant King of myth and legend, rose from her throne and said, "Not *all* the village. Some would not follow a giant. Camber, for example, he and his kind. They may for a while, but inevitably the rage is upon them, and they act against all life. They are of a remnant, and they have left offspring. Those you call the 'Others' are descendant from those beast men of the old Jagged Horde, sons of the blood dragon, Tepes."

Micha and the others looked at one another, then to Docha and the dwarves. Silent, but the puzzled expressions communicated their question. They returned their gaze to the princess. Sighing, she continued, "Tepes' brood? You do not know this story? More I will tell you another time." She flipped her hand, flicking her fingertips dismissively. "Or not."

"Here on the mountain, in the midst of magicks, the encompassing rage of the descendants of Tepes is lessened. You must understand, Camber, you are special, though not in a way that you like. You carry an ancient energy. It is one that my mother helped defeat when I was still young.

"You cannot leave this castle now. You have come of age. For certainty, should you leave, you *will* become like your father. Someone will do to you what you did to him. Perhaps even young Para here, for she has cause and is decisive. Should Para act on her cause, I would grant her sanctuary from human judgment.

"I offer you this choice, fierce Camber. Live out your vision of death and destruction. Return to destroy your village and perish in your youth. Or remain here. Join my small band of warriors. I can use your youthful strengths, and I possess magicks that will keep the beast in you at bay."

Without hesitation Camber said, "I will stay, Princess."

"I can stay too." Tymon stepped forward. "I can fight for you. I am a warrior too."

"No, you are not." The princess strode to Tymon, forcing him to lean far backwards to see her face. "You are a protector of those you care about, but you are not a warrior. You are a poet, a bard, a teller of tales. Your words are braver than your actions, and that is saying a lot, for you show yourself to be quite fearless in the face of my ire."

She turned from him and looked to Persa. The girl was making herself small and peering at the princess from the corner of her eye. As the giantess approached her, she trembled. Tymon made a motion to go to Persa, but the princess held up her hand to stop him. Looking about the room, she appeared to be vexed. Taking a breath, then another, the princess made a decision.

"You are called Persa?" She did not wait for a reply. "I am named Freschia. My father walked with dragons and sought to make all beings better, stronger, more capable. He wished for everyone to have the same opportunities to serve Gaia. He despised one thing. Betrayal. Mostly he despised when people betrayed themselves.

"My father left me, or so I believed. In recent years, I am not so certain that was his intention. My mother left me as well. What her intention was, I have no idea. But they are gone now, and I continue." She took another breath and said softly, "Look at me, girl." Persa did so. "People leave. Days and years leave. Eventually we all leave. You left your village. You chose to go with the people who mean the most to you rather than stay behind. You choose to attend to the ones who support you and you cared for my Lord Tymon One-Eye before he was such. You are in pain at the loss of your father? Then we are alike, Persa. Do you fear I will keep your Tymon?"

Persa uncurled her legs and sat straighter on the large chair. Placing both hands on the edge, she leaned forward but did not rise. "He is my friend, but I am small and weak. If you wish him to remain with you, he will prosper in ways that I cannot imagine or offer. I wish him to be happy, but I wish him to make the choice to stay with you for himself, rather than obey some command."

"And if I command you to stay with me, Lord Tymon?"

Tymon now walked past the princess to Persa. He stood in silence.

"Do not seek to answer now," the princess said. "But know that I will not and never intended to have you remain in this cold castle any longer than necessary. Your purpose is below. There is a future for your people, with or without my aide, and you are now a key to unlocking their potential.

"Both of you, Tymon, and you, Persa. You gazed into the Moon Pool together and what you saw was only each other. You are still young and will understand these things soon enough. Tell your tales together. Tell the stories that carry the best lessons. Let courage be at the core of your songs, and kinship be the theme of your poems.

"You are no burden, Persa. You are wounded. But you are brave enough to face the princess of the castle the best you can. What else are you? At present that is a future unwritten. But you care, and that is why you feel pain at loss. You will heal others because you need to be healed. In this we are alike, though I am the more reluctant and thus you are the more valuable to the world.

"You are not a warrior, Tymon. You are a being who sees beauty no matter how well-hidden. It is enough to be who you are."

************

"Micha, though, he is a warrior, and the best kind. I could ask you to stay, Micha, and your life would be better than any you can imagine. You think before you engage in battle. You see ahead of the course of events. You know when to move and when to be still." The princess sighed. "Yet the Moon Pool showed you something different, did it not? You were standing in your village square, and the crowd was around you willingly. They listened to your words. They prospered. You were not alone."

She turned to Para. "Your vision is a warning. You must not tell it for those who hear will hate you for the fear you bring them. Do not give in to that fear, Para.

"You are young. Never lose that power. Never be less than you are. Always stand for what you feel is correct. Remember, service to others is not the same as being servile. Serve from a point of power. Make others take responsibility for their actions. Keep your friends strong with honesty. You cannot remain with me here. There is only room in this castle for one princess.

"Only Camber may stay. Leaving the castle will be a risk for him. He may do so for brief periods only. He will be my emissary to you. He will bring my word and guidance. I will search out my father's words in his halls of learning and seek to give you the direction you need. Remember, you have asked for guidance. Heed my words well. I am not given to wasting breath on ingratitude.

"I know this, seasons change. Gaia has been in winter long. She has done so before. She will do so again. I can hasten spring. It is why I have lit the lamp. It is a signal requesting aide. It has been answered. Here you are." The princess paused, and her gaze floated from the rapt eyes of the children into the far end of the shadowed chamber. A single red light gleamed in the dark. She returned her sight to the five humans before her.

Her arm swept past Persa, Tymon, Para, and Micha. "You four will stay with me for seven days and nights. I will show you things you will not understand. Practical things, but also ways to witness and observe the world beyond your sight. These next days may leave you confused. Some of you more than the others. I will explain only when I feel it appropriate. Trust that the lessons will be of value in your future. Through this association with me, you will gain strength in a way you cannot understand.

"This is the power of dragons' blood within your veins. It is why you saw the light at the peak of the mountain. The beacon is a call to those of the blood of the true dragons. By your will, by your action, by your ability to see the light, you now have altered your lives and also those generations who follow. The world is often altered in this way. Small stones create widening ripples. Of all the stones Lord Docha has brought to mine presence, you may be the brightest yet. It only remains for you to become polished.

"Lord Docha will take you now, and you will be given rooms. We will meet again at evening meal. After, we will begin your lessons. I will first show you the stars. Best not to begin with the brightest of lights, lest we blind you."

Her manner and tone were regal. Her authority never a question in anyone's mind. Her voice left no room for debate. She was imperious. Now, she lowered that tone, speaking with a faint warmth.

"Lord Tymon One-Eye." The princess laid her long, large, snowy-white hand across his slender shoulders. "I ask that you defend young Persa in the same manner you defended me. You have the heart of a giant. You are released from my immediate service in this matter, and I offer you my appreciation.

"Camber, I ask that you remain with me now."

With that, Docha led the four to the door. With some effort they pulled it open and filed out. The door swung closed of its own accord.

*************

The princess stepped to Camber and placed her hand across his shoulders.

"What do you believe in, Camber? Do you believe in giants and dwarves?"

"I do now, Princess."

"But you believe only because you have seen them? Did you not know of the stories before you embarked in your journey? Did not young Preest tell you of beings who were not human?"

"Yes, but they were stories, and he did not always say they were true. And when he spoke of the great and powerful things they accomplished, and I looked at my own life, and that of the village, it is difficult to see the hand of a beneficial king in what remains of a place once said to belong to him."

"King Kane. That is his name. Or was. I am Freschia, and in time you may say that name as Princess Freschia. But Princess is the better way for now. You believe too that humans can become something...other? You know this to be true about yourself?"

"Yes, Princess."

"This frightens you?"

He nodded yes.

"And what of dragons? Do you believe dragons exist?"

Her questions kept Camber's thoughts off-balance. "I believe the possibility more now that I know you and the dwarves truly exist."

"I have said your companions are of the blood of the dragons. You have heard me say this, yes? And I also say you too are of the blood of one dragon, but it is not a favorable thing. There are dragons, and then there are *dragons*. In my life, the dragons have been as scarce to me as giants and dwarves to you and your village. Yet your people tell the stories and want to believe, want to be rescued. Do you wish to be rescued? To avoid your fate?"

"What about all those things you said? Free will and such? Can I never be strong enough on my own? Will I always be a slave to the beast within?"

"Those questions are unanswerable, good Camber, but the fact that you can ask them says I am making a right decision."

Picking up an iron lantern, she led him to the darkened area of the chamber. The pool of soft firelight cast slender rays from the glass lens. A glinting, mirror-like surface shifted and flowed.

"I, too, possess free will. I, too, am strong. I, too, request assistance." Princess Freschia, standing next to him, now did not appear so tall, so imposing. A sweeping motion of her arm spread heavy curtains further apart. "Camber, this is your new mentor." In the pool of firelight, a dragon stood revealed, red light emanating from its eyes.

The dragon lowered his head to be level with Camber. In a deep and resonant voice, he said, "Greetings, son of a dragon."

# 10

# BEFORE...

THE KING WAS GONE. His magicks remained but were pale and wan. Freschia lived on in the castle, but she had none of her father's abilities to create and connect. Life in the valleys went cold. Visitors ceased their travels. Freschia's travels began.

Lifetimes passed. Once, she became a queen. Once, she rebelled. Once, she fought for her own freedom. Allies were few. Those who remained were loyal in ways she might never fully understand. She returned to the castle and almost failed to find it. Desperation drove her on, for living amongst the fragile short-lived humans was an impossible thought. A mystical realm was formed on an island in the western sea, the place her father perished. She could not go to another's kingdom. Not again.

She sought solitude.

She raged.

She howled in woods, screamed in the forest.

She cajoled, bargained, pleaded with unseen forces, magicks unknown.

She knelt and wept.

One day, hair tangled, clothes torn, tattered, and worn out, hopeless, she simply asked, "Please take me in. Please shelter me." The path to the Cloud Castle opened.

There, Freschia wept alone. The princess did many things alone, but this weeping occurred more often of late. She wandered vast rooms and dark hallways, recalling the warm glow of light emanating from what her father called dragonfire. As a child she delighted in his rare tales of the days of dragons, ancient and wise, the bringers of life to the giants and elves. He did not speak of those days easily. She did not beg their telling. She did recall one dragon. A dragon and his companion, a young girl. She remembered them. Or believed she did.

Only a few beings remained in the castle. Guardians, those bound to her by honor, protecting her from no one. Dwarves, bound to her by her father's final wishes, still brought her gifts. Rubies and sapphires, rare minerals and woods that remained valueless, for there was no one to craft them into fine jewelry, and no one to appreciate how they lay on her fine throat or gleamed in her braided hair.

She knew deep, cold loneliness. Her cries echoed soft in long, empty corridors. "Help. Please help me."

Endless stairways filled the castle. Freschia wondered if new rooms grew, if the magic castle altered and shifted as years crept by. Days would come, and nights as well, when she found herself in places unfamiliar. Surely by this time she had set foot in all places of her home?

A passage, dark and still, appeared at the end of a long corridor. Looking inside she saw the chamber was a tower. A spiral of granite steps, gray and unadorned, curved around the outer wall of a stone tower. Unadorned save for a single carving at the start of the stairs. A picture of a dragon, wings outspread. Beneath the dragon's wing a figure stood. In her life, she had seen few representations of the dragons. They were not forbidden, not exactly. In some books, histories and poems, the princess learned a little of the nature of the dragons. Her father spoke of them rarely and often changed the topic when others raised the subject. She did not ask. Now she wondered why.

Freschia raised her lantern to gain a better sight of the carving. Her breath caught, for the figure resembled herself! With one long finger she traced the image. The tip of her finger felt tiny grit from the grooves, as if the picture had been freshly carved.

The princess climbed. No doors blocked her passage to the wide, circular roof. She stood upon a tower higher than any other of the castle. Surely, she would have noted its existence before? Wind swept up the sides of the mountain. Ice and snow flew past the parapets. Freschia's robes whipped about, and she felt the tight braids of her long, white hair twitch and jerk in the stiff, wintery gusts.

The clouds were heavy, as they were wont to be in those years. Her lantern was lit against the oncoming night. Soft, pale, candle glow flickered against the battering breeze. Candle glow that remained against any breeze, any attempt to be snuffed out. Candle glow that had been lit before her father abandoned her and his castle.

Freschia never thought to question the candles and torches. In all her life, she never replenished the fuel or stoked the flames. That was not the work of a princess. Those who kept the flames lit must do their work when she was not about, she assumed, just as those who cleaned and cooked for her kept out of sight. Not for her eyes were the menial tasks.

At the center of the roof, a wide stone brazier lay exposed to the elements. Freschia could see over the edge and down into the shallow hollow. Neat stacks of wood lay covered in ice and snow, undisturbed for a great many years. She raised her lantern as the sun's light faded behind looming, consuming clouds. She sought to dispel the encroaching gloom. A gust, like a puff of breath, pushed against the flame of her mystic lantern light. Sparks flew. Drops of flame, dragonfire she now knew, sank through the snow and ice. Fluid fire, seeking fuel.

A deep glow came from beneath the drift of white. Shadows danced about the lower hollow of the brazier. Sizzling and crackling, popping and snapping, the snow and ice melted away in steaming puffs of cloud. Vapor rose for some time, then altered to smoke as flame grew to consume the sodden wood.

The princess stood by. Heat and light expanded, and she felt the cold fading. She liked the cold, but for the first time in a great, great while, she recalled being warm. The warmth of her father's arms. The warmth of bodies in motion. The warmth of favored songs and foods shared in the glow of banquet halls.

************

Winter fell when King Kane left the land. Winter fell and never left. Freschia stayed in this frozen world and never wondered of the people below, the visitors once frequent and now vanished. She stayed and carried around the lantern in the dark, never once questioning the source of light.

She cried that her father had forsaken her. Yet...the lantern stayed lit.

Above the world, at a distance, a light grew. From the valley, in the dark, a boy looked upward.

In his heart, he felt summoned, beckoned.

In his heart, he felt hope and did not know what that was.

AUTHOR JEFFREY J. MICHAELS is a Gemini. As such, he is deeply involved in whatever interests him at the moment.

Currently he is polishing a sweeping fantasy series of interconnected tales collectively known as "The Mystical Histories." It is varied enough that he may even finish most of the stories. He likes to think of his work as "metaphyictional," combining fantasy and humor with metaphysical elements.

In his real life, Jeff is a well-respected creative and spiritual consultant.

You can follow The Mystical Histories and his other writings at www.jeffreyjmichaels.com

www.ingramcontent.com/pod-product-compliance
Lightning Source LLC
Chambersburg PA
CBHW061244170626
46809CB00007B/2822